A Dire Wolves MISSION

Savage Sanctuary

A Dire Wolves MISSION

ELLIS LEIGH

Kinship Press

Kinship Press
P.O. Box 221
Prospect Heights, IL 60070

*Thou seest how sloth wastes the sluggish body,
as water is corrupted unless it moves.*

— Ovid

One

winter without snow is bullshit. As is this so-called mission." Levi took a swig of his beer, slamming the bottle onto the table when he was through. The cold liquid soothed his thirst but not his ire. Staking out a rival shifter pack for the umpteenth night in a row was definitely not his idea of a good time.

Mammon laughing certainly didn't help his mood. "You're so impatient. How can you be as old as you are and not have learned the thrill of anticipation?"

And wasn't that the pot calling the kettle black? Although Levi would argue with his pack brother that he did, in fact, have patience, he was sick of spinning his wheels on Mammon's personal obsession. Tired of being forced to stay in the same place instead of being able to roam the way he wanted. The way he craved. But they sat. And Mammon watched. And Levi grew more bored by the second.

Besides, Levi wasn't dumb enough to buy Mammon's

anticipation line. Not considering where they were or what they were doing. Even while teasing Levi about his own struggles with waiting around doing nothing, the big shifter couldn't help but slide his eyes around the bar, probably looking for any sign that the group of shifters across the room was up to something. Up to anything, really. The guy had a hard-on the size of Montana for the newest pack in the area.

Levi would rather get a hard-on for one of the hot little waitresses popping around the joint. "Nothing's doing, man. They are literally sitting there not doing a damn thing, like they do every Friday night."

"Fuck off, kid." Mammon shot Levi a warning glare before going back to doing what he'd been doing…staring at a group of shifters drinking beer. The guy had been obsessed with the crew from New York since they'd first shown up in his town. Granted, an entire pack of big, loud Irish and American shifters appearing out of nowhere and basically taking over the underground business in the area wasn't necessarily normal, but they weren't doing anything to endanger the shifter world. So they fleeced a few humans now and again. There were worse things.

"You need to let this one go." Levi wasn't usually so vocal about…well, anything that went against the grain. But a year of being tied to one place was about eleven months too long—and he was tired of following Mammon's conspiracy theories.

"You'll get your balls cut off, son," Thaus said, probably surprising both men at the table since the two spun to stare at him. Thaus was bigger than the rest of the Dire Wolves, more military, too. In a pack of strategically trained wolf shifters who tended to speak with their claws instead of their mouths, Thaus was still a standout as the silent, broody type.

Of course, Dire Wolves—a breed of wolf shifters long thought extinct by the general shifter population—had never been known for waxing poetic. The legends surrounding them tended to be more based on battles and wars, enemies vanquished and lives saved as they defended their kind.

But Levi had decided long ago that Thaus took that Dire-Wolf-broody persona to a whole other level. The shifter was just…quiet. Unless he was blathering on about military strategy and procedures—then the bastard could go on for hours. Or maybe that was Levi's perception based on his own boredom when Thaus started down that path. He doubted the shifter had spoken enough words to account for *hours* in his entire life.

But Levi talked plenty. "If my balls are all you've got to be worried about, man, you need a little more action in your life."

Mammon snorted a laugh and Thaus raised an eyebrow. That was about as much reaction as Levi expected. Good goddamn, the boredom was killing him.

Levi scoped out the bar again as he finished his beer, not for the other shifters like Mammon, though. No, he was looking for tail. Preferably of the shifter variety. He had the itch to take a shewolf back to his hotel or, even better, into a dark corner of the club and get her on her knees. Maybe a little secret stand-up sex in the restroom. Something. Being stuck in fucking Fort Worth with Mammon for almost a year as they watched a pack of wolf shifters be nothing more than loan sharks and mob-style enforcers had about killed his social life. He needed to get off—and then figure out how to escape this town.

A blonde across the bar met his roving gaze and smiled. Even with the distance and the people filling the space between them, he could sense the human rolling off her. Not his favorite by any stretch, but he could deal. Long legs, short skirt, hair brushing the top of her flat-but-not-unappealing ass. Yeah, he could deal with that just fine.

He sat deeper into his seat, spread his knees a bit, and gave her a head nod in welcome.

Mammon laughed again, the fucker. "Is that the best you got, kid?"

"I'm not your kid, and my style works just fine, thanks."

"Your style?" Mammon bumped Thaus in the arm. "Are you listening to this?"

"I'm trying very hard not to, no." Thaus growled when Mammon hit him again, the bigger man going from broody and bored to downright pissed off. "Hit me again, and I'll take your fucking arm off."

Mammon only laughed harder. That is, until the blonde appeared before them.

"Hi," she said, leaning on the edge of the table by Levi. Tall, sexy, and obviously a little tipsy, she was exactly what he needed for the night.

"Hey. I'm Levi."

She glanced around the table. "Who're your friends?"

"Not important." Levi grabbed her hand, running his fingers over the back of it. "Want to dance?"

"No," she said with a smile, bending at the waist to whisper—quite loudly, really—in his ear. "I want to get out of here."

Her hand was on his thigh, and her breath was feathering across his neck. If that wasn't a sign that she was interested in more than just a drink and a grind on the dance floor, he didn't know what was. He reached down to move her hand higher, giving her a grin.

"I think that can be arranged."

But she wasn't looking at him anymore. She was looking

at Thaus. And that was a huge mistake.

"You look really familiar." She leaned across the table, practically reaching for him, using Levi's thigh for balance. "Do I know you?"

Levi groaned, as did Mammon. Thaus was a lot of things—a good leader, a great soldier, and a badass weaponry expert—but he was not receptive to attention from humans. Nor was he able to control his rage.

Thaus exploded from the table, toppling his chair behind him. Something that barely fazed the other Dires. They were used to him; of course, others weren't. Especially not humans. The girl jumped back with a scream, nearly falling over as she tried to scramble away from what Levi was sure she saw as a threat.

But that wasn't enough for the enraged shifter. "Get the fuck away from us."

The girl's eyes widened, and her fear wafted over the stale, air-conditioned air of the place. Strong enough that even Levi could smell it. "I'm sorry. I just—"

"You just nothing. Go."

So she went, as Levi expected her to. No one could stand up to Thaus when he was having one of his temper tantrums. No one, except maybe Levi himself.

"Thanks for that, jackass." Levi sat back, glaring as the bar patrons stared at the trio, refusing to overreact to Thaus' ridiculous posturing. Not that Thaus seemed to give a fuck.

The bigger shifter righted his chair and sat down hard, leaning toward Levi. Looking ready to beat the shit out of the next person who crossed him. "Look, kid. We've all put up with your bullshit over the past way-too-fucking-long, but I'm done."

And didn't that sound like a bunch of bullshit. "Done with what?"

"You. Saving your ass every time you screw up a mission because you don't pay enough attention. Tracking you down the mornings after you choose pussy over your brothers."

"Thaus," Mammon started, his voice oddly balanced between concern and calm. But Levi certainly didn't need calm, and he had a feeling neither did Thaus.

"Saving my ass? When have you ever saved my ass? It was me who pulled Mammon here out of that building collapse back in Sri Lanka. And it was me who dug through about a thousand pounds of rubble to get to Phego after you sent him into a cave without checking for stability." Levi leaned forward, his growl pronounced under his words. "And it was me who killed the fucking werewolf that almost tore your goddamned arm off."

Mammon sighed. "Guys, we're drawing attention."

But Thaus was too mad to pay attention to Mammon's warning.

"You think you're some badass, kid? You think you can handle a mission on your own? Because out of all seven of us, you're the only one who hasn't, and this shit is why. You just invited over a fucking human during a stakeout on a shifter pack." Thaus sat back as his phone rang, still eyeing Levi with disdain. "Stop thinking with your dick and get with the program before you kill someone."

"Answer the fucking phone," Mammon said, glaring from one man to the other. "Before you two blow what little cover we have here."

"You've been so far up that pack's ass, there is no more cover." Levi grabbed his beer and growled, ready to do more than fight with words, but the warning look on his teammate's face made him pause...and roll his eyes. But he didn't really feel like acknowledging that.

"Go," Thaus said into the phone. The club was too

loud for Levi to hear the voice on the other end. Still, when Thaus stood and strode toward the door, Levi and Mammon followed. Stakeout canceled—time for real work, it seemed.

Centuries of battling every form of supernatural had taught Levi many lessons, the biggest being that sometimes he needed to bite back his pride and do what was needed. Right then, he needed to follow Thaus to find out what the new job was because there was no way the stiffness to his shoulders and the need to go someplace quiet wasn't about a new mission.

When they finally caught up with Thaus, he was standing in the parking lot at a sort of parade rest, listening intently. He looked up as the two moved closer and mouthed the word *Dante*.

Mate of the president of their political ecosphere, Dante was basically their boss. He took the calls from packs who needed assistance, doled out jobs, and made sure the North American wolf shifters stayed controlled and concealed. The dude was like Charlie in that *Charlie's Angels* show. A voice on the line telling them all what to do.

"Are you all there?" Dante's calm voice came through the speaker of the device, his smooth way of speaking hampered by the tininess of the cellular technology.

"Affirmative." Thaus glanced from Mammon to Levi before refocusing on the phone. "Please repeat the orders."

"We've received a call from a pack in Hope Ridge, North Carolina, which is located on the western side of the state. As you may know, that area is rife with human travelers because of the Appalachian Mountains. The pack interacts with the local humans in business needs, but the main property is deep enough into the forest to avoid most human hikers and passersby. They've recently discovered scent trails around the fringes of their land, though. Human scent trails."

"Encircling them?" Mammon asked.

"They believe so, though the terrain makes it difficult to be sure. They're asking for assistance to investigate the issue."

Thaus grunted. "Why are we being called out for a simple human infringement on pack land? Couldn't the local Feral Breed chapter or a few Cleaners handle it?"

Mammon nodded, though Levi didn't care either way. The Feral Breed was the motorcycle club the president of the North American Lycan Brotherhood, Blasius Zenne, used to police nomad and pack wolves. They were usually cool guys—a little on the pack side of things without admitting they were a pack—but they lacked the training of a true military unit. The Cleaners were more tactical and trained, but they tended to be more policelike…if the police were really good at hiding bodies and cleaning up crime scenes to make sure forensic teams never learned of shifter involvement.

The Dires were a different breed and at a different level. If Dante was calling them for this job, there was a reason for it.

And Dante didn't wait to tell them that reason. "The pack has an Omega."

Levi's chest tightened as the pieces came together. Omega wolves were powerful female shifters considered true blessings to their packs. They were rare and coveted, sometimes to the point of obsession. Just the year before, his team had fought in a battle against a group of shifters determined to kidnap Omegas and breed them like farm animals or some shit. The sick bastards.

But on a more personal note than just shifter lore, Omegas were precious to his brothers and him. The all-male pack believed Omegas to be kin, to be the female side of the Dire genes. Something even the legends didn't mention.

The seven remaining Dires in the world made up Levi's pack and worked closely with the political leaders of wolf shifter populations to keep Omegas safe and fight the darker supernatural forms a standard shifter couldn't handle. But the Omega shewolves always came first in their battles.

If an Omega was in trouble, Levi was going to help.

"What's the plan?" Levi asked. Thaus raised an eyebrow, but Levi just glared back. Sure, he wasn't normally one to volunteer for more work, but when it came to Omegas, he felt the need to dive into the action. More so than with any other kind of mission.

"I need a single man to investigate the pack claims and secure the Omega," Dante replied, not missing a beat. "If more men are needed to eliminate the threat, so be it."

Mammon wiped a thumb across his lips, looking distracted. "I could go—"

"No," Levi interrupted, earning another surprised look from Thaus. "I've got this. I'll hit the road tonight."

Dante responded before his brothers could. "Very good, Leviathan. I'll send the coordinates to your phone. Be quick, though. President Blasius does not want another Omega in danger."

Neither did Levi. "Affirmative."

Dante hadn't been disconnected from the call for two seconds when Mammon started up.

"You really think you can handle this alone?"

Levi bit back a sigh. No way would that be seen as mature and capable, even if the irritating old fuck deserved to be sighed at. "I've got this."

Thaus eyed him hard, looking for something Levi wasn't sure he'd find. Still, Levi refused to flinch or look away. Let the bastard look—he could handle it.

But then Thaus spoke. "You fuck up, it's on all of us."

The weight of their ancestry slammed down upon him like a boulder. Dire Wolves…the best of the breed, the strongest, the most trained. Military, focused, and dangerous. Few knew there were any Dires left in the world, and the handful who did would be waiting to knock the legendary beasts down a few pegs. For most missions, Levi chose to act in a team so as not to shoulder that responsibility alone. But this time, he felt the urge to go solo.

"I've got this." Levi stared his brother down, refusing to break.

Thaus glanced at Mammon, then nodded once. "Then you're up."

He headed for his truck without another word, though Mammon hung around.

"I've got this," Levi repeated as he walked, refusing to let the worried expression on his brother's face get to him.

"But your sense of smell—"

Levi cut that shit off with a growl. "My sense of smell does just fine. I realize it's not as strong as the rest of you fuckers after that volcano thing, but it's better than most shifters. I'm not helpless."

"I know that, it's just…" Mammon sighed and ran a hand through his hair. "It's a weakness, and a weakness in battle could lead to a loss that none of us can afford."

Levi wanted to roll his eyes, but he couldn't. He'd burned the fuck out of his nose, throat, and lungs working a mission a little too close to an active volcano in Hawaii a couple centuries back. He'd healed as well as could be expected considering the damage, but his brothers never let him forget that he wasn't quite the same after that day. He could sort of understand it—he'd almost died that day. But his brothers had almost died a hundred times each over the years. No one doubted them the way they did Levi, and it was a serious wedge in their team. At least to him.

"We're talking humans and a pack of shifters looking for backup," Levi said, trying to keep from snapping at the other shifter. "I'm fully capable of handling this."

Mammon nodded, still looking unsure. "What's your plan?"

"Secure the Omega, investigate the scent trails, determine the threat level, call in additional support if needed, and eliminate targets as necessary."

Mammon nodded again before sighing. "Okay, kid. You're leading this one. You keep her safe at all costs, and we'll call it a win." He turned to go back inside the bar before tossing out one final quip. "But keep your dick in your pants. The last thing we need is a pissed off Alpha calling Dante because you got cozy with some shewolf…again."

"It was just one time," Levi yelled before kicking the dirt. Bastards never would forget that. He hopped into his truck, starting the beastly engine with a growl. An Omega was in trouble, which meant it was time to ignore the doubts and the endless memories of his brothers. It was time to get his ass to work.

Two

Amy wiped her hands on her apron and gave the restaurant one last look-over. Chairs in place, tables clean, salt and pepper shakers refilled and sitting beside hot sauce and pepper vinegar bottles, counter shining like a crystal ball, and the smell of fresh-baked breads and muffins floating through the air. Yep. The Hope Springs Diner was ready to open.

"Why don't you finish up with the flowers, then go ahead and unlock the doors, Miss Kelley?" She patted her elderly hostess on the shoulder and turned to inspect her younger waitstaff. Way younger, especially to a shifter like herself who stood at sixty-seven years on Earth. Not that anyone knew that fact. It helped that she didn't look a day over twenty-five. Still, even with what the humans thought of as her age, the girls who worked for her were still younger.

Sandy was just twenty—new in town and looking for a way to make ends meet—while Yvonne was only seventeen.

She would have been in the high school instead of working the morning shift at the diner if it weren't for the huge baby bump weighing her down.

"Ladies, are you ready for the morning rush?" Amy didn't have to ask that question, but the nods the two girls sent her were a relief anyway. "Good. Specials are on the board, and the new menus are in the stack with the others. Smile, be welcoming, and make sure you let me know when Mr. Klaus orders so I can keep his food separate from the rest. No allergic reactions from him in three months. It's practically a record."

Sandy, pencil and notepad at the ready, practically vibrated with anticipation. The girl had a ridiculous amount of energy, which worked out well for her and Amy. "Pot roast sandwiches for lunch, right?"

"Right." The grins on the girls' faces made her heart soar, and a sense of pride fill her soul. "I know. You ladies will make some good tips today."

"I love pot roast day," Yvonne said with a giggle.

"So do the customers." Sandy winked and headed for her section, looking over the tables one last time. She was such a conscientious employee. So attuned to the smallest details. Amy was lucky to snag her before any of the other local business realized what a gem she was. Sandy even took over for Miss Kelley, sending the older woman to open the doors while she finished placing a single flower in the milk-glass vases on each table.

Adding the flowers to the tables was always the last step before opening, and a tradition Amy simply refused to go without.

When the last flower was in place, Amy moved behind the counter to the cooktop. Time to get to work. "Sheriff's already at the door waiting for Miss Kelley. I'll get his eggs going. Yvonne—"

"I know, I know." The youngest waitress rolled her eyes and pulled a pencil from the messy bun on top of her head. "He'll sit in my section and question me forever. Be nice. Smile. And don't tell him to fuck off."

"Precisely." Amy perked up as she finally heard the bell over the door sound. Miss Kelley was a lot of things—sweet, kind, beloved by the entire town—but fast wasn't one of them. That was okay, though. The woman greeted every customer with a smile and a personal comment, and they loved her for it. Which made them love coming here even more.

"Good morning, Sheriff Rodman. Welcome to Hope Springs on this fine day." Miss Kelley's soft, calm voice floated through the dining room, making Amy grin. Hiring that woman had been the best decision she'd ever made. "I heard you had company last night. I'm surprised to see you here so early."

Amy bit back a giggle and peeked over at Yvonne. The young girl had her shoulders squared and a smile pasted on her face. Ready for what she knew was coming. But Amy had a feeling Miss Kelley was running interference for the girl.

"Oh, uh, yes." The sheriff's normally booming voice sure was quieter as he stumbled over his words. "I had a—uh—dinner guest."

"Dinner guest? Is that what they're calling it these days? Why, when I was younger, we called them *casual lovers.*" That southern drawl of hers really accentuated those last two words, something Amy was sure was quite intentional. She choked back a laugh as Miss Kelley sat the sheriff in Yvonne's section, seeing the old lady's plan clear as day. Even Yvonne was grinning.

"Here you go, dear." Miss Kelley said as she indicated

the sheriff's preferred table. "Yvonne will be your waitress today. You remember Yvonne, right? Can't say she'd know much about the whole casual lovers thing. She's been with my cousin's grandson since they were practically babies. Yvonne, when's Billy done with basic training?"

Yvonne placed a glass of ice water in front of the sheriff and gave the judgmental old coot a smile. "One month, two weeks, and four days."

"Must be awful to be separated from your love like that, though I know how proud you are of him for choosing to defend our country."

"Yes, ma'am. It's been his dream since he was a little boy."

"I remember." Miss Kelley shook her head. "And when's the wedding?"

Yvonne's hand slipped down to her bump, a grin lighting up her face. "One month, two weeks, and *five* days."

The sheriff frowned, glancing from Miss Kelley to Yvonne and back. Yeah, a point had been made. He couldn't exactly grill the poor girl about her boyfriend and her baby and her plans for the future if he was out there carousing. Well, he could, and he would again, but perhaps that day he'd go a little easy on her.

Just about everyone in town judged Yvonne for getting pregnant before she was married, which was specifically why Amy hired her. Yvonne and Billy may have stubbed their toes a bit with the whole baby thing, but they were good kids who had a lot of life left before them. The girl needed some money and a skill, though, if she was going to make it outside of Hope Ridge. Amy had been training her to cook, and the kid was good. If she had skills in the kitchen, she could work in a restaurant instead of a bar or worse. The girl didn't want to go to college, didn't want to live a life far from the man she loved, so she'd need to be able to find a job wherever his career took them. Not quite Amy's idea of a happily ever after, but it was Yvonne's life and choice. Amy was just happy she could offer a hand along the way.

As for her, she had no intentions of straying very far from the little town she called home. In Hope Ridge, she was surrounded by lush wilderness, rugged terrain, and the beauty of nature at every turn. The town was tucked into a deep valley, which was situated at the base of the mountain where her pack lived. This place offered the best of both worlds—shifters in the hills, humans down below. Perfection. Plus she had the Hope Springs Diner to run, and she wasn't giving up her business for anyone or anything. Period.

The bell over the door rang again, signaling another guest. Miss Kelley patted the sheriff on the shoulder before turning for the door…but not before making one last dig. "Better be careful, sheriff. Poor Yvonne gets the church glare from half the town because Billy and she did a couple of things out of order. An adult—an elected official, no less—would probably find himself in a bit more trouble than that."

The sheriff coughed, looking decidedly red in the face. "I told you, Miss Kelley. She was just a dinner guest."

Miss Kelley smiled so sweetly at the man. A sure sign she was going in for the kill. "The only thing worse than a liar is a thief, sheriff. Old ladies have trouble sleeping, you know, and dinner guests don't stay over until after three in the morning." And with that, she sauntered toward the door. "Why, Jackson and Tyler Sanders. How's your momma doing? I heard she took a tumble the other day."

Amy chuckled under her breath as she plated the sheriff's breakfast. Miss Kelley certainly was one to make a point, but there was no way you could get upset with her about it. The truth hurt, and all that.

"Order up."

Yvonne hurried over to grab the plate just before the doors opened up and the factory workers who'd been on midnights came strolling in.

"Must be quitting time." Amy nodded toward the doors. "Better buckle up. Looks like it'll be a busy one."

Breakfast ended as the hours passed, and the clock rolled through to lunch. The diner stayed busy even during the transition, though. A sure sign Amy was doing something right after six months of endless work. Thank goodness for that, because if she'd failed at this diner, her father would have dragged her butt back up the mountain and locked her away for sure.

"Crowded today."

Amy looked up as another newcomer to the town, a wolf shifter named Zeke, slid onto a stool. He ate alone and at the counter every day, and he always made small talk with her. Or attempted to, at least. Amy wasn't quite sold on him yet. As the only local shifter who wasn't in her pack, he stood out as something unique. But unique didn't mean better, and a nomad shifter around humans could easily lead to trouble. So far, it seemed he had the skills to blend in with the humans, but who knew how long that'd last.

"Pot roast day; it's a local favorite. How are you, Zeke?"

His smile grew. "I'm good, miss. Thank you for asking. And how're you this bright, winter day?"

"Fine, fine." Amy caught Yvonne's eye and gave her a nod to indicate she should handle the counter patron. "Yvonne will take your order, hon. I need to get in the back and cook if we're going to survive this lunch crowd."

His smile fell, but Amy couldn't worry about it. She

needed to whip up some more mashed potatoes and fast. It seemed as if half the town had already come in for her pot roast sandwiches, and still every table was full. She'd had to call in her backup waitress, a shifter from her pack named Gracie. The woman was practically dancing through Yvonne's tables as the other girl kept the food coming. Sandy was still smiling and working her crowd well, and Miss Kelley had the couple of people stuck waiting engaged in a conversation that left them all smiling and laughing. Things were good… for the moment.

The girls would be thrilled with their tips at the end of the day, she had no doubt. But if she wanted to keep patrons happy and satisfied enough to lay down some hard-earned dollars for her staff, she needed to make sure she had what they were coming in for. Which meant she needed to get her butt off the floor and do what she did best. Cook.

Once she had Yvonne manning the flat top, Amy slipped out from behind the counter. She hurried through the swinging door into the kitchen but stopped short at the sight of a man sitting on her stainless steel prep-area counter. A man who shouldn't have been there.

"What the hell are you doing?"

Benjamin, second oldest in her family, shrugged and continued eating the pot roast sandwich he'd apparently made for himself. "Abel sent me."

Of course he did. If Amy would have growled any louder, the diners would have heard it for sure. "You tell our big brother that I'm fine. I don't need a babysitter."

But Benjamin wasn't really one to care when Amy got riled up. "Tell him yourself. He'll be down here in a few."

The sigh Amy let out was loud and filled with more growl than she cared to admit. She stomped to the stove to pull off the pot of potatoes she'd had boiling for the past half hour. "This is getting ridiculous."

"Tell Dad," Benjamin said with a shrug. As if that would ever work.

"Dad's not going to tell Abel no." She poured the potatoes into the colander, letting the steaming water drain down the sink before slamming the empty pot back on the counter. "Stupid, overprotective, ignorant, immature—"

"Oooh, I know you are, but what am I?"

Amy spun toward the back door where the man in question stood. The sarcastic grin on his face was directed at her, which was definitely a bad move on his part. "You just proved my point, jackass."

"Well, damn," Abel said as he bumped fists with Benjamin. "Someone's testy today."

Understatement…and annoying. "I swear to God, if you don't get out of my kitchen, I'm tossing your sorry ass in the oven."

Benjamin shoved the last bite of his sandwich in his mouth before nodding at his brother. "I'm out of here. Baked Abel doesn't sound appetizing."

Abel didn't seem bothered by their brother speaking and chewing at the same time, though Amy's stomach turned a little. Damn animals, the lot of them.

"You running or driving?" Abel asked the younger male.

Ben motioned toward the back door with his thumb. "Running. I'm not even attempting to get up that deathtrap road until spring hits."

"It's not that bad," Amy and Abel said at the same time. Abel grinned, but Amy huffed and rolled her eyes.

"You two have a good time. Try not to kill each other," Benjamin said with a raised eyebrow and a knowing grin.

"As long as he stays the hell out of my way, he doesn't have to worry," Amy grumbled as she added heavy cream, butter, and garlic to the potatoes. Benjamin let the heavy, metal door slam closed behind him as he left, something that didn't help Amy's mood. Couldn't at least one of her brothers try not to sound like a herd of elephants when they were in her place of business?

"Damn it, Ben."

"Language, sis." Abel shook his head, looking as if he was trying to bite back a grin. The jackass.

Amy shot him her best glare...and stuck her tongue out...right as the door to the dining area flew open.

"Oh, sorry." Yvonne let the swinging door slam into the wall, looking a bit nervous as she glanced from Abel to Amy and back again. The girl tended to get a little awkward around Amy's brothers. Hell, most women did. The men of her family were all big, brawny, and sporting blond curls and blue eyes. Plus, Abel had the best dimples she'd ever seen. Yeah, women loved her brothers. Too bad they were all jackasses...most of the time.

"What do you need?" Amy asked, trying to smile as the girl blushed.

"Oh, uh...I'm almost out of potatoes, and Mr. Klaus just came in and asked if we had any sprouted bread."

Amy hung her head. "He can't have sprouted bread because he's got a gluten allergy. Good lord, is that man ever going to learn?"

Abel pulled the bowl of potatoes from her hold. "Go. I've got this."

But Amy wasn't about to give up. "I don't need—"

"I didn't ask you if you needed help, and I'm not assuming it either. Mr. Klaus *needs* you to make sure he doesn't end up back in the hospital because of his allergies. He's old and he's stubborn and he hates that his diet has had to change so much in the past year. He relies on you to help him. Go. I've got this."

Amy sighed and released the bowl, knowing he was right. "Thanks, Abel."

He shrugged and started mashing the potatoes. "We're family. It's what we do. But don't expect me to leave until you close the door after the last customer. I'm walking you home tonight, missy."

"Fine. But only if we get to stop for ice cream. Your treat."

Abel gave her a grin and a wink, something that probably would have melted a woman not related to him. "You know it."

Amy popped up to kiss his cheek before heading back to the dining room, ready to tackle Mr. Klaus and his ridiculous refusal to listen to his doctors. Another day, another restaurant full of diners. Another dream come true.

Three

ope Ridge sat dark and almost deserted when Levi rolled down Main Street. Closed up for the night—typical of just about any small town, really. In places like this one, the sidewalks practically rolled themselves up at five o'clock.

The Alpha of the local pack wasn't expecting him until the morning. When Levi realized what time he'd actually hit the little town at the base of a mountain, he'd contacted the Alpha and tried setting up a night meeting. Tried… and failed. The man had been adamant that daylight was better—something about mountain roads and darkness not mixing. Still, as much as he wanted to get to work, Levi didn't complain. That delay gave him an evening to explore the snow-covered forests, something his wolf was really looking forward to after so long in Texas.

But first, he needed to find something to eat.

He passed a restaurant on the main strip, but it was

definitely closed. Figuring there had to be more than just the one diner, he circled the few streets that made up what must have been considered "downtown." No luck. Every business was closed for the night.

"Not even a damn bar to grab a beer." Levi drove for a bit, heading farther out of town. Shops and homes blended into fields and woods, which gave way to a factory or two. Then a truck stop and…

What do you know?

Johnnie's Tap Room sat on the side of the road, a dark building with fluorescent lights in the windows calling out some solid American beer choices. There was even a sign advertising their burgers.

"Finally." Levi swung his truck into a parking spot and hopped out. The scent of burnt something permeated the air, thick enough for him to recoil from it even in his human form. Probably some sort of pollution from the manufacturing facilities, though he couldn't be sure. But as he took a step around his truck, Levi also caught the smell of shifter. Wolf shifter, to be exact. That piqued his interest. If the local pack hung out here, he might be able to get a little early recon in before tomorrow's meeting.

As Levi approached the bar, his relief at finding someplace open turned to something closer to disgust. The lot was littered with garbage and broken glass, at least the spots that weren't rutted and cracked. The windows were blacked out, the paint peeling from the walls, and the door halfway off its hinges. The place was a total dive. Inside the building wasn't much better than out—beat-up bar, chipped tables, and worn-out chairs furnished the single room. Not even a pool table or dart board to be seen. Levi didn't normally need much in the way of ambiance, but Johnnie's Tap Room pushed that fact hard.

"What can I get ya?" the old man behind the bar asked, not even bothering to look up at the newcomer.

"Burger and a beer."

"Regular or unleaded?"

Levi didn't answer at first, not until the guy waved at the taps in front of him. Two types of beer. Same brand, one a lower-calorie version. Guess those lights in the windows lied a bit.

"Regular."

The man nodded as Levi took a seat. A beer appeared before him before the bartender headed to the back. Levi figured he was probably off to microwave something that would possibly resemble meat. If he was lucky.

"New blood in town, I see."

The smell of shifter hit him just before a man took the seat next to his. Tall but wiry, the stranger had the look of a nomad. A rogue, if you would. A lone wolf without a pack or a place to call home. Levi wasn't the biggest fan of true nomads—something about not being in a stable pack messed with their minds. True, he tended to live a nomadic life himself, hopping from place to place and town to town, always on the move, but he had a pack. He had the other Dires. He was stable. True nomads had none of that—but the guy appeared harmless enough.

"Just driving through." Levi took a sip of his beer, nearly hissing at the warm swill. "Shit."

The guy chuckled. "Yeah, should have warned you. That whole cold beer thing is a fallacy." He shook his glass, one filled with beer…and ice.

Levi pushed his beer aside. No beer was better than beer on ice. "You part of the pack around here?"

"Nope." The guy shook his head and chuckled darkly. "I'm not really a big fan of group events."

Levi grunted. He'd been right—nomad. Unable to resist, he slipped his phone out of his pocket. If he held it just so, angled it just right, he could get a pretty good profile shot. He needed a picture in case the guy ever ended up the focus of a mission.

Nomads tended to lose control of their humanity over time. The Dires had seen it time and again, but they didn't act unless the nomad became a threat to their world. This guy wasn't a threat as far as he could see—not yet, at least—but he liked to be prepared.

As he fiddled with his phone as if texting someone, Levi was able to grab a good five shots of the nomad from a couple of angles. His team would be pleased. He was the group photographer, had been since he stuck two boxes together and used mercury vapor to develop images more than a century before he walked into Johnnie's. He had a whole collection consisting of pictures of the shifters he'd met over time. Pack leaders, regional heads, important men and women who helped push wolf shifter politics and lifestyle. Taking the pictures had started as a hobby to him. But over the last few decades, his photos had become important to the Dires, so he focused mostly on nomads. The fuckers were dangerous, and having an image of a suspect helped his teammate, Bez, track them down.

Done with his picture sneaking, Levi was about to toss a twenty on the counter and head back for his truck when a pretty woman with a big smile walked up and pressed herself into his side. Definitely human, by the smell of her.

"You order the burger, honey?"

Now that was more his speed. Nice curves, pretty face, and a look in her eye that said she was hungry. Plus, she was bringing him food. Total win. "That's me. Do I get a piece of you on the side?"

Her giggle scraped at his nerves, but he smiled through it. A full belly and a little naked time with a pretty woman seemed like one hell of a way to relax before he started his mission tomorrow.

The waitress set a full plate in front of him, making sure to rub her ample chest against his arm. "I'm Ashley, and I'm here if you need anything."

Yeah, he needed something all right. "I'm Levi. It's a pleasure to meet you."

She gave him a solid eye-fuck before squeezing his wrist. "You come find me when you're through."

Jackpot. "Sure thing, Ashley."

His shifter friend on the stool chuckled softly, but Levi ignored him. He had food, bad beer, and the chance at some pussy. What more could he ask for? Almost bouncing in his seat, he took a big bite of his burger.

And immediately regretted it.

The guy next to him straight up guffawed. "Could have told you that was a bad idea, too."

Levi spat the definitely-not-food into a napkin. "Burgers and pizza are like sex—even when they're bad, they're good. How can something that should be good be so very bad?"

"Bar owner can't cook for shit but thinks he's fucking Guy Fieri. Now, the diner in town? Pure heaven." His eyes got a dreamy sort of look in them, and he shook his head. "Man. Best food I've ever had."

Levi scowled at the thing that was supposed to be a burger. "It looked closed when I drove through."

"Yeah, only breakfast and lunch."

"Figures." Levi shoved the food away and glared at his warm, pisslike beer. The night had gone from bland to horrible in a sip and a bite; not even the promise of a little attention from Ashley could save it. He was done. He'd rather go wolf, do a little hunting on four legs, and jack off in the shower than try to choke down that piece of not-food just to get into a chick's pants.

"Heading out?" the shifter next to him asked as Levi stood up.

He held a hand out to the man. "Definitely. I'd rather chase a few rabbits than suffer this shit."

"There's plenty of those up in these hills." The man shook his hand, his eyes roaming the bar. Before he let go, he leaned in and lowered his voice. "Watch yourself leaving here, all right?"

Great. Just what Levi needed…a cryptic warning from a nomad. "Yeah. Sure. You, too. Have a good night."

The shifter turned back to his beer and nodded, but he offered nothing more. Levi left without another thought, striding through the door into the nasty-smelling air outside. Maybe that stench wasn't from the factories as he'd originally thought. Maybe it was from the owner's attempts at cooking. He could see that since his mouth pretty much tasted as foul as the air after that bite of not-a-hamburger.

"Hey, handsome," Ashley called, appearing like some sort of dream girl in one of his fantasies…or nightmares, really. Could go either way. "Think you can come here and give me a hand with something?"

Levi sighed. His truck was right there, just a few cars down. The last thing he wanted to do was have to jump her dead battery or fix something on her car. But he was a gentleman and had been trained to be helpful and work as a team. Ashley didn't seem to have a team, and who knew what would happen to her if he walked away.

"Sure. Of course." Levi trudged across the broken parking lot cement, hoping whatever she needed help with could be quick. He was no longer in the mood for anything she could offer him.

Ashley was tucked between a car and a larger truck, looking nervous and almost shy. That sent Levi's hackles flying. The chick had practically given him a rubdown. She was definitely not shy.

"What's up, Ashley?"

She shrugged. "Want me to suck your cock?"

Normally, Levi would probably categorize that as the stupidest question ever. Lips on cock was a definite yes. But her placement between the vehicles, the way she was acting, the fact that he couldn't smell anything past the stench of burnt food in the air…all put his guard up. "No, I don't."

Her face fell, and she glanced toward the truck for a split second. Got it…the threat would come from there. Levi edged back, leaving room so he couldn't be taken by surprise from the side or back.

"C'mon," Ashley said, beginning to appear almost manic. "I won't even charge ya nothing."

Oh, fuck. Levi sighed and slid his fingers over the hilt of the knife he always carried, just to make sure it was there. This was definitely about to get ugly. "I'm not interested in what you're selling, Ashley. And if your pimp is around here somewhere, waiting to pull some sort of beatdown on me for turning you down, he'd better make his ass known now. I'm not waiting around all night."

Her face went pale, too pale, and she glanced at the truck again. Levi rolled his eyes and headed for his own truck, swinging wide around the tailgate of the one where he expected a man was sitting in wait. Ashley wasn't a true pro; she'd probably never completed any sort of sexual act with a so-called customer. She was a pawn in a bigger scheme. Drunk men offered blow jobs in the parking lot? Their pants would be on the concrete faster than a flicked cigarette butt.

And that's when the guy would hit, probably roughing the johns up, maybe stealing a wallet. A little cash for basically no work.

But Levi wasn't about to be their next victim.

"Have a good night, Ashley."

"Wait," she screeched, staying behind the bed of that truck but waving wildly. "I can give you what you need, handsome. I do everything."

Levi shook his head and continued walking. What he needed? That was a good meal and an even better lay, followed by some serious running as a wolf. He doubted he'd get any of that in the parking lot of a dive like this one.

"Not interested."

The sound of a truck door opening behind him was enough to pull Levi up short. *And so it begins…*

"The lady's offering you her wares."

Levi didn't even bother turning around. Not yet. "I said I'm not interested."

The click of a gun being cocked changed his mind, though. *This motherfucker…*

Levi turned and dropped his hand to where his knife hung, ready to pull it out at a moment's notice. Phego had customized every pair of Levi's cargo pants so he could carry his combat knife without others seeing it. A tough job to do considering the size of the thing.

"I think maybe you should toss me your wallet," the guy said with an actual smirk on his ugly face. As if he'd already won. As if Levi were some sort of scared little bunny because Smirker there could load a handgun. It would take a perfect headshot to take a shifter down, and Levi was too quick and too agile to give anyone a chance at a shot like that.

The guy had seriously misjudged his prey.

"I think you should take your last chance to walk the

fuck away."

The guy's smirk faltered, but he didn't lower the gun. "What'd you say?"

Levi pulled his SOG from his holster, gripping the handle loosely. Over a foot long from tip to pommel, his SOG SEAL Knife 2000 was his most cherished weapon. Sharp, deadly, and well-balanced, it was a tool made for fighting in close quarters. Some guys preferred guns, some explosives. Levi liked blades. He liked fighting up close and personal. And right then, he really liked the idea of taking this motherfucker down. Gun or no gun.

The guy made another misjudgment when he saw the knife, choosing to laugh instead of run. "Wait. Did you really bring a knife to a gun fight? That's fucking rich, man."

Levi just smiled, waiting. Ready.

When Levi didn't respond, choosing instead to hold the man in a predatory stare, the guy grew antsy. He fidgeted more, the hand holding the gun dropping then coming back up. His feet shuffling a bit. He had no idea how to deal with a man like Levi, which was a pretty normal response. Not a lot of human men would have any idea how to handle a fight with a wolf shifter, let alone a Dire Wolf.

But dumb men made dumb decisions. The guy must have run out of patience, because he glowered at Levi and raised the gun again, looking ready to kill. Levi shook his head and pounced, closing the gap between them in a single bound. That threw his opponent off-balance, which made him drop his arm. The one holding the gun. Again.

This guy had no clue how to actually fight.

Without waiting for the dude to make the first move, Levi slashed his arm with a gruesome downward pull. One cut, and the blood started flowing. Two, and the gun dropped to the concrete. That left Levi's target open for some hand-to-hand ass kicking, though the guy didn't go down easy. He swung hard with his right, only missing because Levi was faster. A good thing, too. Those fists were big for a human.

Levi thrust and dodged, twisting to avoid the punches the guy threw. Big dude followed, off-balance but attempting to hold his own. Both men scrambling over broken footing and seeking the upper hand. Levi doing a better job of it all.

The fight wouldn't have lasted as long as it did if Levi wouldn't have had to keep the gun in his peripheral vision. He had no idea where Ashley had gone, and the last thing he needed was some pissed off pro shooting him in the back. He'd heal—of course—but that would be a bit hard to explain. So he kept slashing, kept cutting, kept landing shallow stabs to the other guy's chest and arms. He wouldn't kill the guy—not yet, at least—but he was definitely going to teach him a lesson.

It was on a particularly deep thrust—right into his enemy's bicep—that Levi heard the sound of another person coming up behind him.

"I thought I told you to watch yourself."

The man from the counter grabbed big, dumb, and ugly and twisted his arm behind his back. Levi took the opportunity to slam the man in the nose with the butt end of his knife, sending him to his knees. A second hit, and the man sagged toward the concrete. Unconscious at last.

"Jackpot," Levi said, growling hard under the word. His shifter friend tossed the guy into the space between two cars, then dropped down to grab the gun. Levi had a moment of pause, a single second where he gripped his knife a little tighter and prepared himself for a second fight, but the guy didn't aim it. In fact, he unloaded the bullets and pocketed them before tucking the gun in his waistband. Smart man.

"Well, that was fun," the guy said, not even breathing

hard. "Where the hell did you learn to fight with a knife like that?"

Levi wiped his SOG on his pants and slid it back into the holster before giving him the simplest and most truthful answer. "War."

That definitely got the guy's attention. "Pack or military?"

"Military. What about you?"

"Pack wars." The guy shrugged, as if that wasn't a big deal. Levi had seen a lot of pack wars over the years, had even been sent in to stop a few. They were brutal, deadly, and downright horrific. If this guy had survived a pack war, he was a fellow brother-in-arms. Period.

Levi held out his arm. "Name's Levi. And I'm glad as fuck that I ran into you tonight."

The guy glanced at his offered arm, then nodded once. He grabbed hold near the elbow, and Levi did the same back, the two holding on for a moment of mutual respect and traditional shifter greeting.

"I'm Zeke. It's nice to meet you, Levi."

The two held arms for a solid few seconds, and then the moment was over. Levi surveyed the parking lot for any sign of their fight that could lead someone back to him. Ashley was gone, not surprisingly, and the big dude was still facedown on the concrete. Otherwise, there was no sign of a struggle. His work here was done.

"So, the diner, eh?" Levi headed for his truck, Zeke following along beside him.

"Yeah. Definitely," Zeke said with a nod. "Hope Springs has got great food and good company. It can't be beat."

"Hope springs eternal in Hope Ridge, apparently. Might have to try it tomorrow." Levi stopped at his truck, ready to go but growing more curious about this particular nomad. "So, you hoping to join the local pack or something?"

Zeke's low growl said just as much as his words. "I'm not a pack dog."

Levi wasn't surprised by the answer—most nomads saw themselves as completely free and weren't willing to go back under someone else's rule—but the fact that Zeke had apparently been in this place long enough to know as much as he did when there was a local pack nearby didn't make sense. A single nomad wouldn't—couldn't—take on a pack. Those odds would never work.

Levi unlocked the truck but didn't get in, leaning on the door instead. "So you're not interested in joining up, but you've been in town long enough to know a few things about the place. Why're you hanging around?"

Zeke shrugged and looked away. "I think my mate's out this way."

Well damn, that wasn't an answer he'd expected. "Ah, then you stay."

"Exactly." Zeke turned back, his eyes filled with a determination Levi rarely saw. "I stay…for her."

That level of desire, of commitment, was something Levi was almost jealous of. He'd never really thought about mates or being mated. His Dire Wolf brothers had all lived as single wolves for the millennia they'd been alive, none of them finding his fated soulmate. Until Dire Bez went on a mission to save a kidnapped Omega shewolf, and the whole world went sideways with a single connection.

Since Bez had brought his fated mate Sariel home with him, Levi had begun wondering what that connection would be like. Not really craving it, but sort of…curious about it. Maybe more than curious. But it had taken a thousand years for one Dire Wolf to find his fated mate. Levi doubted he had any shot of lightning hitting twice. Besides, a mate meant staying put. He definitely wasn't ready to put down any sort of roots.

"Well, good luck, man." Levi pushed off the truck and opened the door, an uncomfortable feeling close to sadness settling into his gut. "I really hope you find her."

Zeke cocked his head, looking Levi over with an odd sort of expression on his face. As if he sensed something different about him. Levi was used to that because there *was* something different. Not that Zeke had any way of knowing he was staring at a legend of the breed.

Finally, Zeke offered Levi a head nod. "Yeah, thanks. It's been a long time coming.

"I bet." Levi hopped into the truck. "Maybe I'll see you around while I'm in town."

"So long as you're not picking fights in parking lots again." Zeke chuckled and backed away from the truck. "And try the diner before you go. I'm telling you, it's amazing."

"Sure thing."

And then Zeke was gone, disappearing into the darkness behind the bar. Probably running off to chase down dreams in his wolf form. Something Levi suddenly itched to do as well.

Instead, he started the truck and threw it into gear. No way, no how. He wouldn't hope for something that would never happen, even if he was in *Hope Ridge*. The sort of disappointment that came from hanging on to and finally losing hope could be soul crushing.

Not on Levi's agenda.

With little more than an inkling and a sense of direction, he pulled out of the spot, turning away from town, even though the pull to go back was strong. Fuck this hope place. He'd head for brighter lights and bigger cities for the night. He could drive back tomorrow for his meeting with the Alpha. No diner was worth falling into the trap of craving what you'd never get to have.

on't let them get to you. Don't give in." Amy repeated the mantra to herself as she drove up the private road that led to her family's land. One hand gripped the wheel of her Jeep as she whipped through the narrow stretch of path through the trees. Most people wouldn't even think of driving down this rutted, dangerous terrain, but Amy did it often enough to know every twist and hole. Too often, in her opinion.

She practically flew over the dirt tracks through the woods, riding out every bump, wanting to get this meeting over with. Why her family needed to call her out for help every few days was beyond her. She had a business to run in town, had a life away from the pack that she enjoyed. She also had twelve strapping older brothers who could handle just about anything. And while they tended to claim they *had* to have her at the pack property because she was *the only one* who could do whatever it was they wanted her to do, she knew they were bluffing. They wanted her to move back in with their parents so they could keep her under their thumbs.

Stupid, arrogant, needy Neanderthals.

When Amy hit the snow-covered field that bordered the pack lands, she couldn't hold back her smile. The mountains were so beautiful up here, even in the grip of a harsh, cold winter. The views were something she missed now that she lived in town. But while the scenery was breathtaking, the pack itself could be suffocating to Amy. Being the youngest child of the pack Alpha and the only daughter of thirteen didn't exactly lend itself to her being seen as an adult. Like, ever.

"Armaita." The voices of the children of the pack reached her just as she parked alongside the pack truck. She grinned as she got out of her Jeep, her boots crunching through the half-frozen snow layer. She didn't even mind them using her full name instead of the more socially acceptable nickname she'd given herself. They were too cute to reprimand for something so silly.

"What are you kids doing out here? It's freezing."

The oldest boy of the group, a dark-haired tween belonging to her cousin, scoffed. "It's not that cold. Besides, the snow is frozen. We're playing don't break the ice."

Ah, the balancing act she'd played against her brothers for years. Played and usually won due in part to her smaller stature. She really loved seeing the disappointment on their faces when the snow cracked under their feet. It was like payback for them being so big and athletic all the time.

"Well, don't go too far, just in case. And come inside if you get cold."

"We will." The kids raced off across the snowy field, laughing and howling at one another. Amy watched them go, a twinge hitting her heart. They were getting big. Even with as often as she was asked to drive out to the pack, she didn't get to see them enough.

But then Abel—her oldest brother and assumed leader of the make-Armaita-come-home party—stepped outside the pack hall building, and that nostalgic, lonely feeling disappeared faster than snow on a warm day.

"About time you got here," he said, crossing his arms and staring down at her with something like ha-ha-told-you-so in his eyes.

Okay, maybe more like snow in hell. "I had a couple of lingerers at the restaurant, plus the road's a mess. I actually had to slow down at one point."

"Chicken." Abel turned and walked inside without another word, something that made Amy grit her teeth. She loved her brothers—all twelve of them—but there were times when they drove her crazy. A lot of time. Like…ninety percent of every day. It was no wonder none of the twelve had ever found a mate. What sort of fate would tie any woman to a man who couldn't—or wouldn't—see past their lack of a Y chromosome to acknowledge their worth?

Don't let them get to you. Don't give in. Amy followed Abel inside, her inner voice whispering her mantra through her mind. She had a tendency to lose herself under the unrelenting power and attitude of her many brothers, especially when her Alpha father got involved. But there was someone even more troubling at these pack meetings, something far worse than her brothers when it came to judgment. Or someone, really.

"The prodigal daughter returns."

Amy ignored the pack Beta, a cousin by the name of Roman, of all things. Unfortunately, the Beta wasn't one to be ignored.

"I suggest you greet me, Armaita. Don't make me tell your father all the indiscretions happening in that restaurant of yours."

Amy closed her eyes and took a deep breath before pasting on her best smile. "I prefer Amy, and it's good to see you, Beta Roman. How's the search for a mate going?"

Roman's phony smile turned vicious, his eyes darkening. "You know damn well that's been put on hold by your father."

"Huh." She tapped her finger against her lips and frowned. "I thought it was your Alpha who put that on hold."

"Same thing."

Abel brushed past Amy, addressing their cousin in her place. "Calling him *your father* instead of *our Alpha* is not the same in terms of respect, Roman."

Roman scowled but gave a nod of his head to show his acquiescence. "You're correct. My apologies to Alpha Bell."

Amy bumped Abel in the shoulder as their cousin stormed off. "I could have handled it."

Abel shrugged, directing her toward their family. "Could have, but why? I've got your back."

"I don't need anyone to have my back. My back is just fine, thank you."

"Did you hurt your back?" Their mother stood, hurrying over to poke and prod her only daughter. "All that standing. You should really get off your feet more."

"I'm fine, Mom." Amy glared at her brother, who chuckled and waved as he disappeared across the room once more. A crowd had gathered in the community house, what looked like their entire pack filling the normally empty space. "What's going on? Why did Dad call for everyone?"

Before her mother could answer, her father stepped onto the dais along the back wall. Tall and strong, he stood ramrod straight, his wild, light hair curling all over the place. Looking so much like a young Robert Redford, he still had women swoon when he walked by. Not that he ever noticed them. He was devoted to her mother, a truly good man who'd led their pack for decades. They may not have been huge or powerful in the world of shifters, but they were a tight-knit group. And they had everything they needed in their little mountain village. Except Amy—she'd always wanted more than her pack could offer her, so she'd moved to the small town a few miles away and opened a business. Bought a house. Started a life outside of her pack.

Much to her family's dismay.

"As most of you know"—her dad's eyes darted to Amy for a fleeting moment before returning to peruse the crowd— "Abel and Roman came across a human scent trail last week. After much investigation, we've determined the scent is not any of the known humans on the mountain. It is a repetitive trail left behind over multiple days, and it is surrounding us."

The crowd grew completely silent, the pressure in the room soaring.

"In order to protect the pack"—again, his eyes flitted to Amy—"we have chosen to call in assistance from NALB president Blasius Zenne."

This time, the room exploded in noise. Never before had they needed to call for protection from the leader of the wolf shifters. The National Association of the Lycan Brotherhood was no simple group, nor were their guards figureheads. They were soldiers, warriors, and they destroyed any enemies who got in their way. Or at least, that's what Amy had always been told. If her father had called on them to help, the danger must be grave.

"What does this mean?" someone in the crowd yelled over the chaotic discussions happening. Her father raised his hands, waiting for everyone to quiet down before he spoke.

"This means we continue as we always do—but with more vigilance. We will have a small patrol guarding the borders until the threat has been contained. Children should remain with an adult at all times, no exceptions." His eyes met Amy's for a third time, though he held her gaze. A sure sign she wasn't going to like what was coming. "And our Omega needs to come home where we can keep an eye on her."

Amy's stomach dropped and her face burned as her entire pack turned her way. This was bullshit. There was no way some human could be a serious threat to them, plus she had a business to run. A business almost an hour away from her pack by the long and winding mountain roads. This threat had nothing to do with her.

She waited for the group to disperse before cutting through the stragglers toward her father. He spotted her long before she made it to him, though he didn't acknowledge her. He was too busy talking closely to Roman, too interested in what his Beta had to say to approach his only daughter.

Too bad she wasn't in the mood to be ignored.

"I'm not coming back." She crossed her arms over her chest when she reached him. "This threat isn't on my doorstep, it's on yours. I'm staying in town."

Roman growled. "Your father has laid down a law—"

Amy snarled a warning. "This is between my Alpha and me, Roman. I'd appreciate it if you minded your own business."

But Roman tended to think with his…well, nothing. He didn't think. Instead, he stepped closer, his hands curling into fists. Threatening her. A quick snap from her father set him right back on his heels, though. Such an idiot.

"That'll do, Roman." Her dad held her gaze as he

motioned for his Beta to leave them alone. Amy returned the stare, Roman forgotten, not afraid of the big, bad wolf before her. Not even when he leaned in and growled in her ear. "You want to challenge me in front of my pack?"

"No, I want to live my life without your interference."

Her dad sighed. "Child, I'm not interfering."

"And I'm not a child."

"Prove it." Abel joined their father, the two men trying their damnedest to get her to break. "Be a mature, responsible woman and retreat to safety until the danger passes."

"And, what? Give up my business? There's no one to run it if I'm not there."

Abel scoffed. "Your business is a pipe dream. You think you're going to be able to keep it up once your mate finds you? Once you've got a pup or two to take care of?"

Amy's back grew straighter, her face hotter. Her words more fierce. "Any mate of mine will accept my independence as well as my need to stay connected to the community. If not, he can truck his happy ass right back to where he came from."

"Children, please." Her father sighed and rubbed a hand over his scruffy beard. "Armaita, I would prefer if you'd come back to the pack for the time being. I don't have the resources to stretch our guards all the way to your house."

"I'm not asking for guards." She put up her hand as both men growled. "The scent trail is around the pack, which means I'm safer in town than here. If I smell or see a single thing that worries me, I'll come back."

"Not good—" Abel started, but a hand on his chest from his father cut him off.

"We can't protect you there, my sweet. Even if we ran as wolves, it would take us a good half hour to get to you if you needed us."

"I know, but there's the sheriff in town if I need something faster."

Abel snorted. "A human sheriff."

If her father wouldn't have reprimanded her for it, she would have rolled her eyes. "Yes, a human sheriff to take on a human problem. What's so wrong with that?"

Abel shook his head and deferred to their father. "She's your kid."

"Yes. She is." Her father gave her a sad smile and ran a finger along her cheek. "She is my child, my youngest, and the most like me of the thirteen of you." He leaned closer to whisper in her ear. "And perhaps my favorite."

Amy grinned. She always had been daddy's little girl, but she'd grown up. She needed her space so she wasn't *only* his baby. "I promise to check in every day and to be vigilant. But I really don't want to leave my business behind to hide out. I can't."

Her father sighed but nodded once. "Fine. But if you don't call, I'm coming down there myself to carry you back home."

"Fine." Amy hopped up and kissed his cheek. "And if I don't hear from *you*, I'm coming up here. Guns blazing."

"Now that's a sight I'd pay to see." He patted her head and headed for her mother, leaving his daughter behind. Sadly, with her irritated brother still by her side.

"This is stupid."

Amy snorted. "I know you are, but what am I?"

Abel wrapped an arm around her shoulders, putting her in a modified headlock. "One of these days, you'll be back on the mountain with us."

Amy escaped his hold and straightened her hair. "Doubtful."

After she'd said goodbye to her friends and family one

last time, Abel walked her to her Jeep. "You good to make it down the hill?"

"Yeah, of course." Amy pulled opened the door, but Abel placed his hand against it. Keeping her from being able to climb inside.

"You know this is a bad move."

Amy saw through that tough-guy attitude, though. Always had. He was worried about her, which she understood. But she couldn't let *his* worry rule *her* life.

"You know I need this," she said, keeping her chin up. "I need my independence from the pack or else I'll go crazy."

Abel stared at her for a long moment before pulling the door open the rest of the way. "I know, which is why I'm letting you go instead of tying you up and tossing you in a closet somewhere. But that doesn't mean I have to like it."

"I know." Amy couldn't resist his sweeter side—even when it was tinged with the threat of kidnapping. She pounced on him, wrapping her arms around his neck and hugging him tight. "I'll see you soon."

His hand landed on her back, and he sighed a sound of defeat. "You'd better."

The so-called road leading to the land owned by the pack was a snow-covered, hole-ridden waste of space that should never—under any circumstances—be called a road.

"Motherfucker." Levi gripped the wheel tighter as he once again felt the tires slide into a rut. Or maybe a hole. Or a door to hell. How the devil did these people drive on this thing?

After another harrowing twenty minutes attempting to navigate his Suburban through trees growing way too close to where he needed his truck to fit, he managed to drive out of the death woods and onto what looked like a field. Covered in ice, of course.

"Wonderful." Gritting his teeth, he drove on at a speed barely above tortoise. His truck still slipped and skidded, even fishtailing at one point. Eventually, after much cursing, tugging, and downright tantrum-throwing, he managed to slide somewhat close to the other cars parked on the ice. Not close enough to be considered in an actual parking space, but enough that he wasn't driving another fucking inch.

When his truck drew to a stop, he threw the Suburban into park and let out the breath he'd been holding for the last two hours. Or at least that's what it felt like. Good goddamn, he was going to have to drive back down the mountain at some point. Unless he could figure out a way to convince one of the pack to do it for him without making himself look like a chump.

Might be worth it, really. Not like he'd ever see these people again anyway.

Once he'd caught his breath and stopped wanting to beat the shit out of whoever had designed that alleged road, he hopped out of his truck, ready to represent President Blasius Zenne, the North American Lycan Brotherhood, and the rest of his pack by protecting this one. Not that he felt all that professional yet. It certainly didn't help that there were a handful of kids on the porch of what had to be some sort of communal building watching and laughing at him.

"Where's your Alpha?"

The kids giggled and pointed behind them before running inside.

Levi huffed and tried to hurry toward the building, his boots slipping a little on the hard-packed, icy snow. "Next time I'm in Texas for the winter, I'm shutting my fucking mouth about wanting snow."

"But without snow, how does one know winter has arrived?"

Levi looked up at the large, blond shifter on the porch. The man was staring down at him with a smile, something that didn't make Levi feel any more relaxed.

"By the calendar."

The man laughed and shrugged. "True enough. I'm

Abel. I assume you're from the NALB."

"Yes, sir. I'm here regarding your human problem." Levi nearly ate it right before the steps, but he caught himself on the railing. What the hell…was this place made of ice?

"You work for Blasius Zenne?" Abel looked him up and down, seemingly unconvinced. Levi was a fighter, not an ice skater for fuck's sake.

"I'm a Cleaner, so, yes, I work for President Blasius Zenne."

A little lie, that Cleaner part, but one that could be forgiven. It wasn't as if he could go around telling people he was a Dire Wolf. Besides, Blasius had created a special force of soldiers called Cleaners to be run by the Dire Wolves, specifically to help hide their lineage. Most packs knew of the Cleaners, and if they didn't, other packs they might reach out to for information would. They were the soldiers of the NALB, and by calling himself one of them, Levi had just tipped his hat that he was not a man to be messed with. Now if he could only get on solid ground so he could stand up straight, he might actually look the part.

Luckily, Abel didn't ask more questions. He simply nodded and opened the door, inviting Levi inside.

His guess had been correct—the structure was a one-roomed communal building. Most packs used them for meetings and celebrations, though some also used them for a schoolhouse or training center. This pack, with their numerous small children running around, likely used it for a school when not needed for meetings.

Abel closed the door behind them and stepped inside. From the back, another door opened and male shifters began to stream inside. Six, eight, ten at least. All blond, all tall and broad. All way too old to be adolescent. The sight hit Levi as odd. Most pack Alphas kicked out their adult males to keep the younger men from challenging them for position. This pack didn't, and that fact would probably make Levi's job much easier.

Or his ability to prove who he was much, much harder.

"You must be from the NALB." A man looking a little older than the rest stepped forward, his scruffy beard and curly hair giving him the look of an aged, hippie surfer. By the way he approached with confident steps, his eyes firmly locked on Levi's, there was no doubting this was the Alpha.

"I'm Cleaner Levi. President Blasius Zenne sent me to assist you in dealing with your human problem."

"You got a team outside?"

"No, sir. Just me." Levi nearly smirked at the doubtful expression on the man's face. "I'm more than capable, but my team will be called in should the threat be more than we think."

"Well, I guess you'll have to do," the Alpha said with a sigh that almost made Levi growl. "I'm Alpha Zuriel Bell. Allow me to introduce you to my sons."

The man turned, giving the other towheads a nod. They all lined up in height order, Abel as the tallest at the head. Levi looked down the row of men once more, seeing the resemblances. The son aspect made sense, but good lord, what a huge family.

"This is Abel, Benjamin, Caleb, Darkon, Eliezer, Felix, Garab, Huram, Israel, Jeremiah, Kenan, and Lucas. And this man on the end is my beta, my nephew Roman."

Levi nearly laughed. "Bible names for your kids and a Roman for your nephew. Interesting contrast."

"My brother thinks he's got jokes." Alpha Zuriel moved to the head of the line, the biggest and strongest of the males in the room. Excluding Levi. "Being that we're so close to a human travel destination, we're quite accustomed to running across them in the woods or occasionally on our property. But this is different."

Right to work…Levi respected that. "I understand you found a scent trail."

Zuriel nodded once. "We did, and it circles our pack lands."

"Fully?" Circles…as in surrounded. As in a net. Shit.

Alpha Zuriel's brow lowered and the expression in his eyes grew hard. "As fully as one can get without falling into the gorge on the south end, yes."

Being surrounded wasn't good. Though humans couldn't really fight at the pack's level, they could still be a danger. Shifters weren't easy to kill—pretty much only massive blood loss or a shot straight to the head would do it. But they could be captured, experimented on, outed to the world as something that actually existed. That was the last thing the NALB would ever want to have happen.

Levi needed to figure out why the humans would be out on this cold mountain, stat. And why they were surrounding the pack.

Levi had to ask the obvious question. "Could they be hikers?"

Alpha Zuriel huffed. "Not likely."

"Not possible," Abel added. "Hikers wouldn't circle us multiple times or slowly move in."

"Move in?"

Abel glanced at his father. "They're getting closer."

Levi's mind spun with strategy and attack options. If the humans were close, there had to be a reason. Government operatives who knew what was in these woods, hunters who didn't, sick bastards assuming this group of people in the middle of the forest were humans and, therefore, easy prey—all possibilities.

All things he was trained to deal with. "I'd like to check it out for myself."

Abel nodded. "I'll take you."

Levi followed him through the back door and out onto a porch. The door opening to the outside was on a hinge that allowed it to be opened with a shove from either side, and the wall leading to the main hall was lined with baskets of cloaks. Levi'd seen this sort of setup before.

"Shifting space?"

Abel cocked a smile. "We had to add it on when a couple of our cousins mated to humans. Those women sure are shy about skin."

Levi chuckled. In a world where clothes didn't shift with you, nakedness was a normal part of life. "What about you? Been lassoed by fate yet?"

Abel's smile fell. "No. None of my siblings or I have found our mates."

Oh. Levi stripped quietly, folding his clothes and placing them on a bench along the back wall. Twelve sons and no mates. Not unheard of but, still, odds were that at least one would have found their fated match. If they ever left the mountain.

"What about your pack Omega?" Levi said as he readied to shift.

Abel shook his head. "We'll swing by her place on the way back."

"She lives on the fringes of the pack?"

"Not exactly." Abel shifted, curling from two legs to four in a heartbeat. Levi followed, shaking out his fur before racing the other wolf through the door and across the snow.

The land rolled through forests and past rivers, rocks and trees breaking through the blanket of white to lend shadows and depth to the scenery. The icy ground was easier to navigate on four legs. Levi's paws spread with every footfall, his claws breaking through the hard top layer and finding purchase with each step. He inhaled the cold air in greedy gulps. This was what he'd been missing—the cold, the snow, and the feel of winter in his lungs. Heat in the summer months was fine, but winter was meant for wolves in heavy fur coats.

They ran all day, sniffing and searching out any signs of humans. Finding plenty. For hours, they investigated the wilderness around the pack, Abel leading Levi through woods and over hills. The shorter day worked against them, as darkness crept across the land far sooner than either of them probably wanted. There was more to search, newly found trails to follow, but night was already on its way.

They circled along the edge of a deep gorge, skirting the drop-off and coming up over a ridge. The view was amazing, the sunset making the entire sky glow in oranges and pinks. Levi would have enjoyed the sight longer, but the unmistakable scent of human male seeping from under the snow caught his attention. The scent was heavier, darker, more concentrated than the others they'd found. This was a crossing point, a place of congregation. A meeting spot.

Time to go to work.

Nose down, he led Abel down a new trail, weaving in and out of the brush along the slight path heading east. The scent was stronger still, the men having obviously walked it multiple times recently. Hikers, maybe. But the terrain was rough here, the path barely visible, and the cold harsh. If the ones going through were hikers, they were awfully extreme. Yet there was no sign of climbing or camping, nothing but a path worn through the snow and foliage.

Definitely something not quite right going on.

As they came to a split in the path, Abel tried to head

north. Levi guessed that path circled the pack land, but there was another scent trail. Weaker, perhaps older, but another path leading away from the pack. Something in his head, some whisper of instinct, told him that trail was more important. He yipped and headed along the new scent path, slowing down to a quick walk to keep from losing it. Definitely newer. Fewer men had followed this path, maybe even only one. This was a private path, a secret road to something important. He knew it…felt it in his bones. *This* was the scent trail that would lead them to answers.

But as they came upon the crest of the hill overlooking the far edge of a small town, Abel began to growl viciously. Head down, hackles raised, he looked like a beast ready to attack. An impressive sight to be sure. Levi, though, had no clue why, or what had set the wolf off.

Needing answers he couldn't get with growls and chuffs, Levi shifted to his human form, crouching naked in the last bit of gray light before darkness swallowed them. Abel followed, the two breathing hard as they peered toward the lights of three small houses in a row.

"What's doing?"

Abel growled again, pointing. "That's my little sister's place."

Levi followed the man's finger to the dark house on the far right of a string of houses below. Something about it called to him, but he couldn't pinpoint what. "The lighter scent trail I picked up continues that way. Maybe the men are watching her as well."

"Fuck." Abel stood and began to head toward the house, something entirely not in the plan.

"Hold up, man." Levi jumped in front of him, stopping him in his tracks. "We need to get back to the pack lands before we do anything down there."

"What? I'm not leaving her undefended." Abel growled and tried to shove past him, but Levi wasn't budging. Not on this. His instincts were firing rapidly, telling him the house was the place to be, but he would not screw up this job by giving in to instincts. He knew the plan, and he would make it happen.

"My instructions are clear," he said, pushing the words out to convince himself as well as Abel. "If a threat is present, secure the Omega, then call for backup. Obviously, my team needs to get their asses out here, but I have to secure the Omega before I call them. My only mission is to keep her safe. That's what I'm going to do as soon as you take me to her."

The need to investigate the house intensified, a form of worry or fear building in Levi's gut. Something unlike anything he'd ever experienced before. *Mission first, then house. Secure the Omega, then explore the situation with the little sister.* He couldn't fail this, couldn't let his brothers or Blasius and Dante down.

He would *not* let an enemy snatch this pack's Omega.

Abel huffed a laugh, though, practically ignoring Levi's declaration. "You'd better head this way with me."

"I told you—"

"No, I told *you* that's my little sister's place," Abel interrupted, growing louder and more forceful. "What I didn't tell you is that she's our pack's Omega, and she lives alone."

Amy's meat loaf was quickly becoming her second-biggest seller. The diner had been busy all day; not as busy as a pot roast day, but steady. She'd have to try another comfort food item for a special next week. Maybe chicken-fried steak or roasted turkey. The holidays were long gone. Her customers could be missing those fall smells. Definitely something to think about…after she closed up for the night.

Almost an hour after she'd flipped the open sign to closed, there were still people sitting in the booths and at the counter. A sure sign she was doing something right with her business. This tiny, vintage building where she'd set up shop had become her favorite place to be, too. It was where she felt the bonds to her community grow and strengthen. Where she felt she had a voice, an opinion that mattered. This restaurant was her home, and the customers her own tiny, mixed pack.

Humans and shifters alike visited her little diner in the

mountains. The shifters stayed polite and calm, not wanting to upset the humans or the daughter of the local Alpha. The humans…well, they were a bit clueless about the genetic makeup of the people scattered around the cozy restaurant, but that worked in their favor.

There were five men at various seats when Amy grabbed the coffeepot for one last fill-up. Well past closing and still they sat, reading papers and books, staring at phones, or just holding on to a coffee cup and watching the snow-covered world go by outside her large front windows. She couldn't decide if she should sigh or smile, though her lips were already pulling up. This was what she loved, the taking care of people, the building relationships and making new friends. But it had been a long day, her feet hurt from walking about forty miles over the tiled floor, and she really wanted to go home.

"Last call, gentlemen." Amy circled the tables, heading for the few occupied seats. "Sheriff? One for the road?"

"Yes, thank you." The big, burly man sat back to give her room to pour. He'd been coming to the diner since the day she opened, and she knew he was a huge reason why the other residents in town flocked to her as much as they did. Shifters tended to make humans nervous—the whole "no longer the top of the food chain" instinct kicking in when they met. But the sheriff had been unafraid, and he'd put the townspeople at ease with his casual acceptance of the place. He may have rubbed her the wrong way with his treatment of Yvonne, but Amy would always be grateful to him for helping her get started.

He took a sip and hummed his appreciation. "Good coffee as always, Amy. And the meat loaf was excellent today."

She couldn't have held back her grin if she'd tried. "Thank you. It's a family favorite, as well."

Big mistake, mentioning the family. She knew better than that. She was about to move on to the other customers, escape while she could, when he sat back. The look on his face, that inquisitive, searching stare, was not what she needed right then.

"How's your family doing?"

Amy's smile faltered, but she tugged it back into place. Sheriff Rodman had always been a bit curious about Amy's kin up in the woods. Lots of townspeople were, really. And while Amy could see how her family's life could be viewed as unconventional by human standards, she didn't always like the tone people used when asking. They'd start off curious but end up almost accusatory. As if choosing to live a life away from the vast majority of the population was somehow wrong.

"They're good, sir. I was just up there the other day, visiting."

He nodded and took another sip of his coffee before continuing. "Must be difficult reaching them, what with the amount of snow y'all have gotten up there. Where exactly is that road to the property? I don't think I've ever seen it."

And there it was—the digging, the curiosity, the slight look of disbelief in his eyes. Sheriff Rodman had been trying to get information about her family's place ever since she'd moved into town. Too bad for him she knew what he was up to.

"You'd never see it. My brothers really need to clear that entry a bit more." *Not that they ever will,* she added silently. Amy didn't miss a beat in the conversation, though, giving him a smile as she changed topics to one she knew would get her packlands off his mind. "I've got some meat loaf left over in the back. Would you like to take it to the station? It's way more than I could eat, and I'd hate to see it go to waste."

The sheriff rubbed the back of his neck, trying really hard not to look as excited as Amy knew he was. "Oh, I couldn't do that. Why don't you take it home? Feed whoever you've got coming around."

More digging. He always did have to mention her living alone and the potential…company she might keep. But Amy kept smiling, confident she could throw him off the scent.

"You take it to the station. I'll put a couple of plates together with mashed potatoes and green beans. Give those young men you just hired a solid meal for one night." She leaned down and lowered her voice as if whispering a secret. "There's even enough for you to take a plate home yourself. Meat loaf for breakfast is one of my favorites."

The sheriff paused, the look in his eyes going from questioning to plain old hungry, and then he nodded. "I'd be much appreciative, Miss Amy."

That was enough for her. She escaped his attention and hurried to the back to grab the leftover meat loaf from the refrigerator. Doors were slammed a little too hard, and the knife she chose to use to cut the slab of meat was a bit more than she needed. Not that she gave a shit about all that. Not at that moment.

Whoever you've got coming around.

"It's whomever, you jackass." Not that there was anyone to hear her correct his grammar. Or any *who* or *whom* knocking at her door. There were no men lined up to take her out. She was too tall by human standards, too heavy. And any shifters who came through the area were usually well aware of who she was. Or more importantly, who her father and twelve older brothers were. Her bed was as cold and empty as could be. But heaven forbid a woman live in a house all her own, one she purchased with her own money. She just might lose all sense of propriety and do silly things like have relations with men and—oh, the horror—have a real life outside of her work.

The knife made a satisfying thunk as she slammed it through the meat. Stupid, arrogant, overprotective men. She'd left twelve of them behind when she moved away from her pack—thirteen, if she counted her father. She certainly didn't need the sheriff's attention.

Once she'd delivered the meat loaf to the sheriff and wished him a good evening—breathing a sigh of relief when he left without another inquisition—she grabbed her coffeepot and headed for the last few stragglers, determined to have them out the door within thirty minutes. It was well past time to go home.

"Coffee?"

Gavin, the new kindergarten teacher in town, looked up from his book and smiled. He had beautiful eyes. A light almost-jade color that complemented his fair skin and hair. He'd be snatched up by one of the local single ladies in no time, Amy was sure. Especially being a teacher of such young children—the very concept of a handsome man with a heart for little ones was like catnip to the female population. But right then, he was looking at her. Smiling at her. And she just may have blushed because of it.

"One last cup if you don't mind. I'm at the good part in this book and want to finish before I head home."

"No problem." Amy poured his coffee and hurried off, needing a little room to breathe. The man was adorable, nerdy and sexy at the same time in that way few men could pull off. He was also not her mate. As unlikely as it was for her to even meet her mate in a town this small, she still held out hope. She'd grown up watching her parents be deeply, madly in love with one another. She wasn't willing to settle for less. And while Gavin might be fine for a night or two, there would be no future for them. So she'd flirt and harbor a little crush on the kindergarten teacher. And she'd wait for her mate to show up.

There was one last customer in the restaurant by the time Amy made it around the counter. He'd sat in the same spot every day for the past week, ordered the same food, and smiled at her with the same dark eyes. A nomad shifter named Zeke, the one who claimed to be passing through town.

"Want a warmer, Zeke?"

The shifter shook his head, holding up his cup. "This is good. Thanks."

Amy was about to head to the back to wash out the carafe when Zeke leaned forward over the counter and dropped his voice.

"Really? The schoolteacher?"

Amy's face grew warm, and she glanced toward Gavin before leaning closer. "That's really none of your concern."

Zeke shrugged. "I just figured a strong female like yourself would go for someone a little more…like us."

"Not that it's any of your business, but what I go for is not that human. Gavin's a nice man and fun to chat with. That's all."

Zeke grinned and gave her a wink. "Good to know."

Stupid, arrogant men. Why was her world filled with stupid, arrogant men? "I don't go for drifting shifters, either, Zeke, so why don't you head on out to wherever it is you've been holed up? It's getting late, and I want to go home. Alone."

"Have a great night, Amy," Gavin called from the door as he wrapped his scarf around his neck.

Amy stepped to the corner of the counter, putting a little space between her and Zeke. "You, too. Take care of those little ones tomorrow."

"I'm out as well." Zeke stood and tossed some money on the counter. "It was nice chatting with you, Armaita."

And that was how he went from just a stupid, arrogant man to an asshole. "My name is Amy. Only my pack calls me Armaita, and you're not pack."

Zeke laughed. "No, I'm certainly not that."

He left without another word. Without reaching for a coat, either. Stupid shifter. While the cold might not bother him once he shifted to his wolf form, the humans would notice a man without a coat out walking in weather like they were having. He was going to make people suspicious.

Ten minutes later, she donned her own heavy, wool coat, flicked off the last of the lights, and headed out into the falling snow. The town was blanketed in the cold, white stuff, the rooftop lights of the open businesses glowing happily beneath it. Main Street in her town had a charm to it few could rival, especially not in the current economy. But Hope Ridge had survived the big-box stores creeping into the area and the everything-for-a-dollar craze. Hell, they had even flourished a bit with the increased tourism in the area. Their business center was filled—not a single empty storefront— which was a fact Amy was proud to contribute to.

The walk home was something Amy loved, especially with the snow coming down. It was as if she were walking through the middle of a snow globe, one shaken up to make the owner grin while watching the glitter fall to the bottom. Her Jeep was awesome, but there was nothing like strolling the streets of her little town. People were friendly here, and the houses were beautiful. Even on her own block, with nothing more than three little saltbox homes side by side, the charm of the place radiated.

Her cheery red door greeted her when she mounted the

steps to her porch, the glass dark. She must have forgotten to leave the hall light on. She unlocked the door and let herself in, tossing her keys in a bowl on the foyer table and turning the lamp on. Golden light bathed the wood floor and pale walls, giving the place a homey glow. Amy sighed.

Home at last.

She hung up her coat, kicked off her shoes, and headed for the kitchen. Not that she was going to make an actual meal. Cooking all day had worn her out, though she was a little on the hungry side. Time for her go-to… Popcorn and red wine for dinner sounded amazing.

But as she turned the corner into her kitchen, a shadow that didn't belong caught her attention. She flicked the overhead light on…

…and screamed.

It took Levi a good four seconds to be able to speak after Abel dropped his truth bomb.

"Your Omega doesn't live on pack property?" What the hell was wrong with this pack?

"I know." Abel tugged on his hair, his claws appearing and disappearing with each breath. He was obviously having a hard time containing his wolf. His growl had become a long, subtle sound—almost a yearning. This was a man too close to losing control, but Levi wasn't about to coddle him.

Levi's anger, his years of fighting to protect Omegas, his memories of missions gone wrong, all came to a head and zeroed in on one already upset shifter. "You *know*? That's the best you can do? *You know*? You don't know shit. You have no idea how dangerous that is even in the best of times. The things shifters will do to get and keep an Omega—"

"I know," Abel roared. "You think we didn't consider that? Fuck, man—you've never met my sister. Armaita is as stubborn as the day is long and just as independent. She wanted a life outside of our pack, separate from her Alpha father and twelve older brothers, and there was no dissuading her." He sat in the snow, staring hard at the little house below. "She came to my dad with an idea to leave the pack and start her own business, so we agreed on this plan. He let her move out here to town, close enough to keep an eye on. And we have—kept an eye on her. One of us is always close by when she's working, and we loop through from the other end on our patrols at night. We watch her, man." He sighed, still sounding like a wounded wolf in a human body. "She is the light of our pack, the glue that holds us all together even when she's not there, but she wanted more than just hiding up in the mountains. She would have left for good if we wouldn't have given her what little freedom we could."

Levi bit back a snarl, still too worked up to find a way to truly control himself. Sariel, Kalie, Angelita…the names slammed into his head like the resonating blast of a gong. All Omegas. All kidnapped and forced to live realities no one would wish on their worst enemy. Thankfully, all recovered from their captors. Though the Omegas they lost were the ones that hurt the most to think about. He did not want to add Armaita Bell to that list.

He wouldn't let this Omega become a forgotten one.

"We need to get her out of there. Right now."

Abel hopped to his feet, looking ready to attack the unknown threat. "What's the plan?"

"I call my team to come in and hunt the humans down."

"And my sister?"

As much as Levi hated to say the words, he had to. There was only one way to be sure she'd be safe. "I take her with me, and we hide."

Abel's eyes went wide, and his voice was filled with doubt

and judgment as he spat, "You *hide?*"

"Yes, *we hide.*" Levi stalked forward, crowding the shifter against a tree. "I said it before—protecting the Omega is my number one priority. And right now, protecting her means getting her the hell away from whoever happens to be monitoring all of you. If they're trained, they'll use her isolation to cull her from the pack. If they're not trained, her living alone is the perfect opportunity to do a snatch and grab. Either way, she can't stay out here alone, and until we know who's watching the pack and why, she's not safe with you, either. Omegas are powerful and coveted—I need to get her the fuck out of the path of whatever's brewing here."

Abel shook his head, but his expression turned to one of worry as he looked out over his sister's house. "She won't go willingly."

And wasn't that a rub? Kidnapped for good or kidnapped for evil, either way, she was about to have her independence ripped away from her. Preferably by Levi. Immediately.

"Too fucking bad. No independent shewolf is going to keep me from doing my job, especially not when that job is keeping her alive."

A woman in a long, thick coat turned the far corner and headed toward the house in question, making both of them stop and stare. Levi couldn't keep his eyes off her, couldn't look away even for a second. Something about her slammed into his wolf and nearly knocked him to his knees. She had to be the sister, the Omega. That magic within her was working some serious mojo on him, had him all hyped up and ready to race down there. Be the knight on the white horse or whatever.

Abel confirmed Levi's assumption. "That's her."

"Let's go." Levi shook off the snow that had collected on his hair and shoulders, shivering as the wet liquid hit his warm skin. "I'm freezing my balls off out here."

But Abel didn't move, just watched his sister as she walked farther along the street below. "She's going to hate us both for this."

"Let her." Levi brushed off the internal whine of his wolf at that thought. "I'd rather your sister be alive and hating us than dead and not. Or worse."

Abel glanced at him, confusion heavy across his brow. "Worse than death?"

That question ate at Levi, made him remember things he'd rather forget. Things he'd seen. Things he'd been too late to stop. "There are many fates worse than death, especially for a young female."

Abel blinked twice before realization seemed to fall over him like a blanket. His eyes went dark, dangerous, and the snarl that left his lips was positively vicious. "Hide her."

"That's the plan." One that needed to happen… immediately. "You meet her inside and get this shit rolling. I want to check the perimeter of the place. See how close our peeping toms have come."

"On it."

The two men shifted without another word, Abel heading straight for the back porch of her house as directed. Levi ran across the yard to the side of the house, following the subtle scent trail. The newly fallen, heavy snow was an excellent camouflage, and his damaged nose certainly didn't help that situation. But he was determined. He tracked hard, using every bit of his skill and senses. Following the scent all the way around one side of her house, right up to the window at the far back corner.

There were no other houses on this side of hers, no neighbors to see someone peeking inside. A definite possibility considering how concentrated the scent was underneath the window. Levi's gut knotted at the possibility of what room that spot looked into. He hoped it wasn't what he thought…but his wolf was already growling in his head. Teeth out, claws ready, the beast confirmed what Levi knew even before he looked inside. Still, he hopped onto his back paws and peeked through the glass.

Bedroom—of course—because no way could this situation *not* get any creepier than it already was.

The scent was on the window ledge, on the glass, even on the siding of the little house as if the creeper had rubbed up against it. Scenting the place. The proof that the person tracking the girl had obviously stood outside her bedroom window and watched her do any number of personal things made Levi want to set fire to the world. He wanted to rip out the throat of the unknown peeper, wanted to break through the window and stand guard over the woman he had yet to meet. His protective instincts were screaming so loud inside his head, he practically did just that. But the thought of scaring her, of breaking in to her house like an animal and making her fear him, helped him keep control. If only for a moment.

Clinging desperately to the thread of human sense that told him he had to be cautious in how he approached this woman, he ignored his wolf's need to kill and hopped down. It was time to get her the fuck out of town.

He'd made it halfway around the back of the house when the deep quiet of the winter's night was broken by a scream. A woman's scream…coming from inside. Levi was running before that scream ended, hightailing it across the snow to the back porch. He hit the door at full speed, slamming his body into the wood. The obstruction cracked and flew open…straight into the wall behind it with a crash that nearly shook the little structure.

Levi had a brief moment of observation—of Abel standing in the kitchen with a cloak covering him—before the woman screamed again and jumped back, focusing on Levi for one heart-stopping moment as he skidded to a stop. That was all it took.

Everything in Levi's world tilted as the realization forced him to stand as still as a statue. His axis adjusted to accommodate the woman into his frame, to pull himself into her picture. A feeling he'd never had before wrapped around him, one of concern and care, one of belonging. One of fate. Without knowing her, he felt the pull. She was so much more than just another woman. So much more than a shewolf, an Omega, or the daughter of the local pack Alpha. This tall, curvy female with light eyes and smoky blond hair staring back at him was everything. She was his fated mate. His one and only…

And she was in danger, which meant a slow, deliberate courtship was completely out of the question. He was about to kidnap her with her pack's permission, which probably wasn't the best way to kick off a long-lasting relationship with an independent woman like her.

Shit.

Eight

my screamed when she saw the man in her kitchen, nearly shifting wolf to protect herself. But the light hit him at just the right time, illuminating him just as she felt the telltale prick of fur sprouting from her skin. Just as she realized who the intruder was.

"Christ on a cracker, Abel. You almost gave me a heart attack. What the hell are you doing here?"

Her brother growled in a tone that made the hair on the back of her neck stand up. Silent, practically looming over her, he stepped closer. Boxing her in. Looking angry as hell but saying nothing.

"Abel?" Amy took one small step in his direction just as the back door exploded off its hinges. She screamed again, falling backward into the cabinets. As she slid to the floor, her eyes met those of the wolf standing in her ruined kitchen. A huge wolf with claws and teeth that made her want to run away. But something deep and dark swirled in the depths of those eyes, something tinged with a color close to silver. An unusual combination she'd never seen before. An intense connection she'd never felt building in a heartbeat.

Mate.

She landed on her ass, completely lost within her own head. Her mate was there. At her house. Standing in her kitchen as if he couldn't move a damn muscle. Staring at her after having broken through the door.

After having broken *down* her door.

"Shit." A stranger in her house, when she normally would have been alone, was nothing to sit back and take lightly. Luckily, Amy was quick to react, even after the whole mate thing boggled her brain.

She jumped to her feet and grabbed the first substantial object she could find—a heavy, cast iron skillet she used for cornbread, which happened to be sitting on the stovetop. Without pausing for an explanation, she made one leap in the wolf's direction. He shifted just as she touched down, leaving her with the impression of dark curls, dark eyes, and holy hell muscles. But she was too focused on defense to really get a good look at him. He'd invaded her space, broke in without asking entry, and could have planned any number of horrible things for her. The bastard. She'd show him what happened when you messed with a shewolf.

Even with Abel yelling her name, she didn't deviate from her target. She tightened her grip on the skillet, swung her arm wide...

And crashed the heavy pan into the side of the man's head.

"What the hell are you doing?" Abel rushed past her, kneeling by the naked man on the floor. The naked man with the very nice ass...not that she was looking. Much.

"He broke in."

The man groaned, one hand holding his head as the other kept him on his knees. How he wasn't unconscious after the hit Amy delivered, she didn't know. That hit probably would have killed a human.

Abel looked at her as if she'd lost her mind. And maybe she had, because she could not take her eyes off the guy's ample rear end. Even with her brother right there in the room. Did stranger-man have a magnet in that thing?

"He's from the NALB." Abel sighed and cursed under his breath. "He's here to help us."

Well…what? "Oh."

"Yeah, oh." Abel patted the guy on the shoulder a couple of times. "Levi, you okay, man?"

Naked guy—Levi, apparently—only flinched and growled at first, but he eventually lifted himself off the floor and sat back on his heels. His eyes darted to meet Amy's right away, and that feeling of connection rushed back in. For one tiny moment, the two stared at one another. Falling deeper into the mating haze. Bonding.

But then those dark eyes refocused on something behind her, swirling to silver in a single breath, and his wolf made itself known. The growl he let loose shook the cabinets and made Amy scuttle back to get out of his way.

"What the fuck?" Levi groaned and grabbed his head. Abel raised his eyebrows as if to say, *See? This is all your fault.* And it was…it really was. She was never going to live this down.

"Sorry, man." Abel sat back and sighed. "My sister thinks she's a badass."

"Shut up," Amy hissed. As if she didn't already feel like crap for knocking her mate unconscious. Oh my God, her *mate*.

Abel snorted, yanking her from delusions of love at first

sight and happily ever after to the reality of an older brother who'd never grown up. "Make me."

"Oh, that's mature."

"For fuck's sake. I have too big of a headache for this shit." Levi shoved off the floor, a little shaky but at least able to stand on his own two feet. He glared down at her, the look almost harsh. "Are you the Omega?"

Before Amy could answer, Abel jumped in. "This is my sister, Armaita."

Bastard. "I go by Amy."

"But her name's Armaita."

"Abel, quit."

"Make me."

Her sigh was big enough to be heard by the neighbors. "Really? Are we doing this—"

"Enough." Levi grabbed a cloak from the basket on the back porch and tossed it around his shoulders. Covering all those beautiful muscles. Pity, really. "Amy, Armaita, whoever…pack your shit. We have to go."

She was still contemplating all those dips and planes hidden by fabric when his words sank in.

"Excuse me?"

Abel stepped in. "The pack is being watched, as are you, so you're going with him to get out of the way for a few days."

"Like hell I am."

But Levi didn't seem to want or care about her opinion. "Whether you're willing or not, you're leaving town with me now. You decide if it's voluntary or if you'd rather be thrown over my shoulder."

That image had possibility, but not in the way he was planning. "I'm not some child who can be—"

"Someone's been spying on you," Abel interrupted.

"They've been here. At your house."

Amy spun, her eyes going wide. That fact changed… everything. "What? Who?"

"We don't know who. The scent is male and human." Levi stepped in front of her, the cloak barely covering all the best bits of him. A total tease, and one that did nothing but make her angry. But he held out a hand as if to introduce himself, his eyes swirling back to the dark color. His expression softening just a bit.

An emotional wizard, that's what he was. She sighed and took Levi's proffered hand, but he didn't shake hers as she'd expected. No, the asshole had to yank her up and over his shoulder, tossing her around like a sack of potatoes.

"Put me down," she yelled, pounding on his back. He ignored her, though. Striding toward the front of the house as if her opinions didn't matter. Though she guessed, in this situation, they probably didn't. He had to be the soldier guy from the NALB. He was probably used to sweeping women off their feet—literally—and doing as he pleased. But not with her…not in her house. She'd rather die first.

She growled and let her canines descend, ready to take a piece out of his hide, but then he stopped. And he sniffed. And he snarled.

Now, what?

Growling, he set her down on her feet and gripped her shoulder. "We don't know who's been here, but you do."

Amy tucked her hair behind her ears and crossed her arms over her chest. "What are you going on about?"

He inched closer, invading her space, nuzzling into her neck. Sniffing her. Scenting. And by God, was it hot. She stood completely still, too afraid to move. Too afraid not to. Her legs shook, her heart raced, and every inch of her cried out to this one man. This sexy, strong, virulent man.

This man who wanted to steal her away without asking if she approved. The fates really had a wicked sense of humor.

"You smell like him," Levi whispered, his lips fluttering across her skin.

Amy jerked back, meeting his eyes. Watching them swirl from dark to silver and back as he growled. Falling into their almost hypnotic pattern. "What?"

"You smell like him." He leaned in again, this time stopping millimeters from her lips. "This peeping tom fucker was close enough to touch you today."

Nine

The bastard might have touched her.

The scent of men on his mate's skin—particularly the one who'd been taking in a show outside her window—worked Levi's wolf into a frenzy. Thankfully, he wasn't some young pup who couldn't rein in his beast when needed. He had experience and skills, patience earned over hundreds of years. He could settle himself.

Most of the time.

It didn't help that Amy, his *mate,* for fuck's sake, was staring up at him with those wide eyes of hers. Jesus, she was so pretty. All tall and thick and sexy with curves for days. He wanted her all to himself, but that wasn't possible yet. Not with everything else going on.

But he couldn't resist completely. He growled and sniffed her again, pressing closer, feeling the warmth of her skin against his. He needed to pull himself away, to grab clothes instead of this ridiculous cloak. Loose fabric did nothing to hide the burgeoning problem that was his cock liking his mate a little too much. But it was hard. Both the pulling away and his cock. So fucking hard. Fucking…yeah.

Damn it, he needed to focus.

"You can…smell him on me?" Armaita, or Amy, as she preferred, was trying so hard not to stare. Her eyes kept flicking from his face to his shoulders to someplace farther south. He liked the farther south dips the best.

But her brother had followed them into the living room, and she wasn't letting on that they'd formed any sort of connection. Which was fine, really. Levi was about to pack her up and take her away from here for at least a few days. They had time to explore their connection. And each other. Lots of exploring to do along those curves and dips.

Fucking focus.

"The scent of male on you is too strong to hide," Levi said, his voice growly and deep. A tone he couldn't remember ever actually using before.

"Who is it?" Amy glanced at Levi as he shrugged.

"Not a scent I recognize, but I'm not from around here. Abel?"

Her brother strode forward, pinning her in place with his hands on her shoulder. For a long few seconds, he sniffed all around her arms and hair, her neck and hands. She held still, the seconds passing like hours, her eyes locked on Levi's.

But her brother only sighed when he pulled away. "They're too many scents for me to break any one out."

"Go outside," Levi ordered. "Sniff by her bedroom window then come back and try again. Maybe that will help."

Her brother rushed back down the hall toward the kitchen, leaving the two of them in the sort of silence that carried a weight with it. Tense, she would have said if she'd dared to open her mouth. Of course, Levi didn't say anything, either. Just stood there, staring at her. Making her tremble with that intense look.

She'd never been happier to see her brother walk through the door as the moment he came in from outside, though she kept her eyes locked on Levi's. Might as well enjoy the view.

"Okay. Let me try again." So Abel did. He tried sniffing for another long minute or so, but in the end, he pulled back with another sigh. "I just can't tell."

Amy's eyes cut to her brother, a daring sort of smile curving her plush lips. "Not the best tracker around now, are you?"

Abel huffed. "Still better than you."

"Can we cut the bickering for a minute?" Levi rubbed the side of his head, wishing the ache there would disappear a little faster. Shit, his mate really packed a punch with that skillet of hers.

Amy's eyes tracked his movements, her face curving into a frown when he pulled his hand away with blood on the fingertips. "Grab me a clean towel from the linen closet, would you, Abel?"

As soon as he left the room, she regarded Levi with a serious expression. "I'm not leaving like this."

He hated pissing her off, but he hated the thought of her being in danger even more. "Pack your stuff."

Those light eyes of hers flashed, a spark of anger flaring bright. "This is my home. My business is here. I can't just walk away."

The sadness creeping into her voice gutted Levi, but there was no way he was fucking up this mission. Not when it had just turned so personal.

"You have to come with me. We need to keep you safe from this guy."

Abel returned with a white hand towel. Levi nodded his thanks and pressed the fabric against his aching head, noticing with glee the flash of concern on Amy's face.

"How do you even know this person is bad? Maybe he's just…curious?" Amy crossed her arms over her chest, drawing Levi's gaze right to her cleavage. Her soft, full cleavage. Good God, his kingdom for some denim. He changed his stance to hide the way his cock was tenting the cloak, hoping like hell Abel hadn't noticed. But even with the distraction of her ample breasts and his aching cock, he couldn't hold back his protective streak.

"Curious enough to watch you through your bedroom window?"

Amy paled. "What?"

"What?" Abel jumped into the conversation with a booming voice. One Levi understood too well at this point. The world was filled with sick bastards.

"His scent was concentrated outside the window." Levi had to clench his hand into a fist to keep from reaching out when her expression went to one of pained horror. And it was only going to get worse. "He'd been out there multiple times. My guess is for long stretches of time."

"That's it." Abel brushed past the two of them, his growl deepening. "I'm packing your shit now."

As soon as he left the room, Amy refocused on Levi. And she didn't look thrilled. In fact, she looked both heartbroken and incredibly angry. "How do I know you're the safe one?"

He cocked his head. "You *know*. You feel it the same as I do."

His heart nearly skipped as she nodded, all slow and reluctant. Yeah, she knew they were mates, all right. But even so, she needed encouragement. And he was going to make sure she knew where he was coming from.

"Even if we weren't—" he stopped, licked his lips, avoiding the word they both knew would have to be said at some point "—even if we weren't *connected* the way we are, you'd be safer with me than anywhere else. My brothers and I protect all Omegas. That's our job. It's our calling." He stepped closer, unable to resist the draw to her. Wanting to feel her skin against his. Craving her touch as he'd never craved anything before. "I would never let anything happen to you."

Her eyes stayed on his, her face giving nothing away. But then she inched closer. Her shoulder brushed his, barely even a touch, but it was enough to set his soul on fire.

He stood stock-still as she clutched at the side of his cloak. Clinging to him in a way. They were two stars drawn together by gravity, seeing the eventual crash but unable to avoid it. Not wanting to, really. He couldn't wait to crash into her.

Finally, Amy sighed. "Fine."

The win wasn't as sweet as he'd have liked, though. She sounded defeated, and that wasn't something he wanted from her. But before he could figure out what to do to calm her, Abel rushed back into the room with a black duffel bag over his shoulder.

"Get in your truck and go."

Levi never had been good at taking orders from men who had no right to give them. "My truck's up on that mountain. We'll take hers to start."

"You leave your keys in that beast?" Abel asked.

Levi nodded. "Front floorboard, driver's side."

"I'll call Caleb and have him drive it to Markson's pass. You drive her Jeep and switch out there."

Levi held in his relieved sigh, grateful but not wanting to show too much excitement. At least, this way, he didn't have to attempt driving down that mess of a road. Let those who knew it best traverse the thing. "That'll help to confuse anyone watching her, too."

"Yeah, that's what I figured. Though, they could be watching her car." Abel paced the length of the room, growling, looking like a man trying to figure out how to solve a calculus problem. "I'll get Benjamin to come down, too. Just in case you need interference."

Levi wouldn't dare turn down extra help, not when his mate was the target. "I'd appreciate it. You keep this fucker off my tail, and I'll keep her safe."

Amy scoffed. "The *her* in this is right here."

Well…damn. Two minutes into his mating and already pissing her off. Levi shifted his weight, letting his shoulder brush hers again.

"Trust me," he said, grinning. "There's no way I'd forget that."

She ducked her head, something close to a blush darkening her face, taking her from adorable to sexy-as-sin in two seconds. He wondered how far that blush would spread. If it would drop to her chest, color the tops of her breasts. Work its way down the creamy flesh to darken her—

"Yo." Abel talking into the phone snapped Levi's attention back to the present and his eyes away from his mate's…assets. Amy was watching him, though. Looking more afraid than he would have liked.

"I'll keep you safe," he whispered, giving in to his desire to touch her with a single finger along her wrist. "I will always keep you safe."

The tension between them grew thick and heated, the two practically leaning into one another for support. There were so many things Levi wanted to say, to do, but first on his list was to get her the hell out of this place until his brothers could figure out who the threat was.

Abel hung up and caught Levi's attention. "He'll be there in twenty. You'd better get on the road."

And so it begins…

"I'll call my team from the car," Levi said, taking the bag from Abel.

Amy took a deep breath before she popped up and hugged her brother. "Be safe."

"Shouldn't I be telling you that, squirt?" Abel smiled at his sister then shot a much more serious look at Levi. He reached out and grabbed forearms, offering his respect. Something Levi didn't take lightly. "I'm holding you personally responsible for the safe return of my sister. Anything happens to her, and I'm taking it out of your hide."

The weight of what Abel and his family were trusting him with settled over his shoulders, but it wasn't something he couldn't handle. When they learned of the mating, they'd understand how there was no way anything bad was going to befall Amy. Levi would rather die first.

"No worries, man. I've got this covered."

His truck was way too big, yet Amy couldn't shake the feeling of being trapped. She was alone with a shifter she didn't know, confined with a man the fates threw into her path to join with forever, heading off to some unknown destination to hide out from a threat of some unknown danger. Alone. Mated. In danger. Her world had become one giant plate of slop in a matter of minutes while she stood in her kitchen.

And he was so very silent.

"So…" Her brain floundered with that single word, stuttered in a way. Nothing else popping up to finish any sort of question or statement to fill the awkwardness.

The man—Levi, like the jeans apparently—tossed a look her way. "So?"

She tugged at her skirt to cover more skin, hoping to get more comfortable. Trying and failing in the most miserable way. "So."

And nothing. Not a single word to add to "so." Not doe or crow or tow or flow. Just nothing. What a way to start off on the right foot with her mate.

They rode in silence for what felt like hours as she racked her brain for something to say, something to ask. Something more meaningful than *where'd you come from* or *where are we going* or *how can you be so fucking hot.* Especially that last one. She couldn't ask him that. Oh God, what if she did? What if her brain got so tangled up that she lost her verbal filter and asked this man how he could possibly be so handsome? She'd have to throw herself out of the truck. She bit her lip and looked out the side window, just to be ready. They were driving fast enough that she'd definitely be injured if she jumped, but they weren't over any mountain passes or deep gorges. She'd probably survive the fall.

"Are you always this nervous?"

Amy jumped and spun, speaking without thinking. "I'm not nervous."

His laugh immediately made her regret that particular answer.

"I'm sorry," he said, giving her a smile that nearly melted her panties. "You looked as if you were contemplating jumping out of the truck. I figured I was making you nervous."

Amy glanced out the window, frowning. "That's ridiculous."

He tapped his fingers on the wheel, staring out the windshield. Amy sighed, wishing she could settle down inside. It couldn't really be her fault that she was so upset. It wasn't as if she'd been prepared for any of this. Who could possibly be ready to be scared out of her wits, meet her mate, and find out some freak had probably been jacking off outside her window as she lay in bed and ate ice cream?

Because that's all she'd permit herself to think about when she imagined some faceless stranger watching her. The thought of him seeing…other things was too mortifying to allow.

But all that was secondary to her current conundrum. She didn't like the tension between her and Levi, but she wasn't sure how to end it without just biting the bullet and digging harder for something to say. So she took a deep breath, closed her eyes, and said the first thing that came to mind. No fucking filter.

"I don't even know your name." She cringed. "I mean, your full name. You're Levi…like the jeans."

She groaned, barely suppressing the urge to once again calculate the trajectory if she chose to throw herself from the truck. But Levi didn't laugh, he didn't scoff either. No, he answered her with a voice so deep and dark, it spoke to her in some sort of primal way.

"I'm Leviathan, though my brothers are the ones who nicknamed me Levi. They felt it was more…modern."

The grateful sigh that left Amy was followed closely by her smile. This was a conversation she could have. "You have brothers?"

He frowned, his eyes still on the road ahead. "Sort of."

Or maybe not. "How do you sort of have brothers?"

"We're not exactly related…not the way most people would think. I mean, we are, but…it's a long story."

The fact that he seemed nervous as he stumbled over his words helped Amy finally relax a little. "Seems as if we have some time ahead of us, and I like stories."

He threw a smile her way. "Yeah, we do have time. But I want to know about you first. You said you have a business."

The swell of pride when her diner was brought up was something Amy had long since gotten used to. "Yeah, the Hope Springs Diner. Breakfast and lunch only, though my customers tend to feel comfortable enough there that lunch sometimes runs into the dinner hour."

Levi shook his head, grinning. "Of course."

"Of course what?"

"I met one of your customers last night. He had to tell me three or four times to go to the diner." He glanced her way for a moment. "You must really enjoy what you do."

"Totally. I like standing on my own two feet, and the diner makes that possible. Even though my brothers hate it."

He chuckled low. "They do seem a bit—"

"Brutish? Overprotective? Ignorant of how capable a single woman can be?"

His chuckle made her heart skip a beat. "I was going to say concerned about you."

"Yeah, well. That too. But I can take care of myself."

Levi pointed to the side of his head. "I'm fully aware of that."

He met her eyes for a tiny moment, a single blink in time. But she liked it. Liked what she saw there, liked that he seemed to want to look at her. She could see herself liking so much about Levi.

She turned her entire body to face him, cuddling into the corner between the seat and the door. "I have a feeling I might be the first woman to hit you upside the head with a skillet."

He grinned but kept his eyes on the dark road ahead. "Definitely the first, and hopefully the last."

There was so much meaning in that statement, so much more happening in the conversation than skillets hitting skulls. She found that fact oddly comforting, like secret messages telling her everything would be okay.

Amy closed her eyes, letting the sway of the truck put her mind at ease. It had been such a long day already, and they still had many more miles to go. If she could just rest for a few minutes, she'd be fine.

"Thanks for saving me," she murmured, trying hard to keep her eyes open. But the lull of the rocking truck and the monotonous sound of the wind and road flying by were almost too tempting to resist. She was suddenly so very tired.

Levi glanced her way before turning up the heat. "Get some sleep, Amy. I'm not done saving you, but we're safe for now."

"Safe is good. Safe…with you…" She had no idea if she said the words or just thought them.

Eleven

When Amy finally fell asleep, Levi dropped the easygoing attitude. He'd been trying to hide his worry beneath a smile and some good conversation, not that doing either of those things was difficult with Amy around. She was funny, a little quirky, and downright interesting. But she was also nervous, and he didn't want to worry her more by letting her see mission-Levi. He'd had to sneak looks in the rearview to check for headlights, had to monitor traffic while also trying hard to concentrate on her, had to ignore the pings on his cell from his team as they moved closer to her pack.

This whole being mated thing was trickier than he'd thought it would be.

He checked the rearview again for any sign of a tail. Finding the road behind him dark and empty did nothing to ease his mind, though. Their getaway had gone too smoothly, been too easy. He was completely unable to relax even without a direct threat, but he wasn't sure if it was the mission as a whole or the Amy-being-his-mate part of it that was making him so edgy. Not that it mattered, really. He needed all threats to her eliminated. There was no way he'd relax until his brothers figured out what the fuck was going on and made sure it was clear to bring her back home.

Her home, not his since he didn't officially have one. Had never wanted one. And shit, wasn't that going to be an interesting conversation at some point? Especially when he admitted he was a breed of wolf long thought to be extinct. One that had been feared even by their own kind at times throughout history. That'd go well for sure.

As he crossed the border into West Virginia, heading for a safe house he knew and particularly enjoyed, his phone buzzed with an incoming call. At the same time, Amy sighed in her sleep and shifted forward to a position lying down on the seat, her feet now pointed at the door and her head… Shit. As if her sprawled beside him wasn't bad enough, now she had her head awfully close to where he'd like it to be.

Quit thinking with your cock.

He swiped to answer the call via speaker and turned down the volume. "What's doing?"

At the sound of his voice, Amy snuggled closer. Rested her head on his thigh, her hand just above his knee. And fuck his life, he could feel her hot breath through the fabric of his jeans. His cock positively ached for something, anything. Some kind of rub or kiss or friction. He shifted his hips to attempt to move into a more comfortable position and took a deep breath. For the first time in his very long life, he was going to have to talk mission stuff with one of his brothers while sporting a hard-on. Wonderful.

"We're halfway through Alabama," Mammon answered, throwing a tiny cupful of ice water over his raging libido. "Where are you?"

Even as distracted as he was, Levi knew better than to be specific over the phone. "Heading to a safe house. Dante has the coordinates."

"Good, good. Make sure you let us know when you're there. How's the female?"

Said female sighed and clenched her hand on his thigh, squeezing him. Levi coughed back his growl and shifted in his seat again. Fuck, his zipper was not helping the pain level of his cock.

"Fine. She's…fine."

But she was so much more than fine.

Mammon sighed. "Please tell me you're not going to do your usual and try to get in her pants."

"Negative," Levi bit out, his irritation with his brother nearly enough to counteract the fact that his mate's head was basically in his lap. Nearly, but not quite. Getting in her pants was not exactly where his mind was at right then. "I'm full mission."

That was an outright lie, and the first he'd ever told to Mammon, but the bastard would understand once he knew the full situation. Once Levi told all the Dires about Amy being his mate. They'd accepted it when Bez had found his mate Sariel; they'd accept Amy. But he wasn't ready to let that little secret out of the bag just yet. Once they knew, the boys would be on them like white on rice, knowing the mating imperative would cause Levi to lose focus. They'd charge in and try to take over, to keep the two of them apart. That just wouldn't do. He wanted them far away for the moment. At least until he actually acknowledged her as his mate for the first time.

Fuck, the timing on this could *not* be worse.

"Right." Mammon didn't sound convinced. "Look, man. If you decide to fuck her, at least be discreet about it.

We don't need some backwoods pack flying off the handle because you can never keep your dick in your pants."

Levi snatched up the phone, taking it off speaker with a growl. "Jesus, man."

"Try to deny it, kid. Arizona, California, Alberta, twice in Ohio…and those are just the recent ones. Remember that time you started an all-out pack war in Brazil?"

"That wasn't my fault—how the fuck was I supposed to know she was some token virgin sacrifice? We didn't even speak the same language." He blanched, hoping like hell Amy had slept through that. He'd never been ashamed of his behavior before, never really given it much thought, but now… Well, now he had a mate. And that fact changed everything, including how he saw his past behavior. What had he been thinking?

Mammon snorted a laugh. "Point proven. Just behave for a few days, okay? We'll be pulling up on pack land in a couple hours. Don't make me have to dig for excuses for your playboy ways, and don't fucking embarrass us."

"Whatever, jackass." Levi ended the call and tossed the phone into the slot under the radio. He was completely screwed. True, he liked the ladies. He liked them a lot and always had, and they certainly seemed to like him in return. But that didn't mean he couldn't accomplish his mission.

Plus, Amy was more than just some random. She was his mate, his fated partner. The days of casual sex for the sake of it were over. With a single look, he'd become a one-woman man, and he couldn't wait to get to the safe house so he and Amy could begin building some sort of friendship. Or something. He hoped for more than friendship, much more, but he'd go at her pace. She was his angel, his piece of heaven, and he would never do anything to ruin that connection. He also would never do anything that would put her at risk.

As he turned off the highway, Amy sighed and rolled. Her forehead rested almost perfectly against his cock, her hand on his hip. She was safe, warm, comfortable, and making him practically weep with need. The perfect combination of heaven and hell, right in that moment. If Levi was being honest, he had to admit he wanted in her pants—absolutely—but that wasn't all he wanted. Not even close.

He wanted so much more. So much that he'd never given a second thought to. He wanted everything with her.

But first, he had a few hours of driving to do to get her out of the danger zone.

Twelve

The little cabin in the woods seemed charming but oddly terrifying at the same time. Amy was alone… with Levi…who was her mate. The man she knew almost nothing about. *Alone.* They would be in close company for a couple of days, he'd said. *Alone.* Just the two of them in this quiet, quaint little cabin that looked as if it had been pulled right from some sort of dream honeymoon catalog.

Did she mention they were going to be alone?

She had to get her mind off of…things. Dirty, sexual things. The sorts of things that would make a few days alone with a handsome, sensual man fly by.

"You coming?"

Amy jerked, looking up to find Levi standing on the porch with the door open. He had a smile on his face, one that made her heart race and her panties wet. This was it… time to head inside and figure out a way to survive the next few days without throwing herself at him. Not until they'd figured a few things out, at least.

Taking a deep breath and praying she had the willpower to resist him, she walked into the house. Her shoulder brushed his as she passed him, and he released the sexiest, most heart-stopping growl she'd ever heard. She wanted to live in that growl, to hear it against her skin. Feel it between her legs.

Willpower…destroyed.

Still, she managed to walk deeper into the house even as her legs shook with the power of her need. Managed to walk past him without throwing him down on the floor and straddling those thick thighs. Or his face.

Being alone with him was going to kill her.

The inside of the cabin was just as adorable as the outside, warm and inviting with a golden glow to the few lights dotting the space. Homey. It almost seemed wrong to look around and imagine all the possibilities for sex on the cushy furniture. And the slick tables. Even the rocking chair ignited her imagination. She was officially a goner.

"Who lives here?" Amy ran her finger over the table by the door, trying to determine if it was strong enough to support her weight. It was a good height, but the spindly legs probably couldn't take the abuse of a man like Levi. Though, she could just bend over and use it as support. That position had possibility.

"I do…sometimes. I like the Appalachians."

Amy spun, having totally forgotten she'd actually asked him a question. Levi froze, his nostrils flaring, holding on to the door as if it were some sort of life preserver. Shit, there was no way to hide the level of arousal she was at. Not from a fellow shifter.

Swallowing down the humiliation of knowing he could *smell* her, Amy asked, "You…own this place?"

His stare made her knees weak, and the darkness of his eyes wasn't helping. She didn't know if she wanted him to mention her need or not, didn't know if she'd rather he acknowledge it or ignore it. All she knew was she wanted him to keep looking at her just like that. And maybe, just maybe, come a little closer.

"No." His voice came out more wolf than human, more growl than not. And she liked that…a lot. "President Zenne owns this place, but my pack is allowed to stay in any of his properties in between missions." Levi finally crept closer, his eyes holding hers in their grip. He paused next to her, not leaning in, but close. Really close. Enough so that his arm brushed against hers, making her shiver. "This is just a place I come back to when I need time alone. The mountains are stunning, the place is quiet, and there's a peace I find here that doesn't come from anywhere else. It's…comfortable."

Amy swallowed hard, staring up at him. Trying so damn hard to control her breathing. But his voice enticed her, his closeness aroused her, and the truth behind his words nearly made her light-headed.

"You brought me to your home."

His growl was softer this time. Deeper, though. "I don't have a home."

But those words didn't ring true. Not in the least. Good God, the man had brought her to the place he considered his den. Neither of them had said a word about the mating bond, and yet there they were. Dancing around it. In the space he saw as his own…even if he wouldn't admit it.

Levi gave her a soft smile before sniffing one last time. With a sound like a groan rumbling through him, he brushed past her, his steps slow and reluctant. Amy took a deep breath and leaned on the little table. This being alone in the woods for days was either going to be the best or the worst decision of her entire life. Death by sexual tension…it was a serious possibility.

She watched as Levi disappeared around a corner, her eyes on the way his jeans hugged his hips. But then he turned on a light and what was obviously the kitchen appeared from the darkness at the end of the hall. A kitchen with dark wood cabinets and stone countertops, it looked like. With that warm, homey glow of the rest of the house. Her space… her favorite room in any house. She was too intrigued not to follow him.

And boy, was she glad she did.

The kitchen was a mix of modern and antique, the perfect blend of wood, steel, and stone. It was also a chef's dream—large counters, professional appliances, a well-placed island with a prep sink built into it—everything set up for speed and reduction of steps.

Amy had never coveted a kitchen more. "Prettiest thing I've ever seen."

"I've seen prettier." Levi's soft growl had her turning to face him. He stood on the other side of the island, staring at her. Devouring her with his eyes. Just as she'd coveted the kitchen, he was coveting her. Her pulse jumped, blood pounding through her veins. She wanted to live in that look, to dive into the green of his eyes and stay there forever.

But Levi stole his gaze from her, giving a small cough as he shot an almost confused glance around the room. "Yeah, so… I don't use it as much as I'd like to."

Amy took a deep breath to recenter herself outside of Levi's orbit. "You cook?"

He checked that each window was locked before turning for the back door. "Barely. I warm."

"Ah." That made sense, though the idea of cooking had her wishing for something to eat. She never did get to make herself dinner. "Do you have supplies? Food of some kind?"

"There're non-perishables in the pantry, and the freezer should be stocked. It usually is."

He disappeared around the corner, checking every access point as he went. Even only having known him a few hours, Amy noticed the hard set to his shoulders. He was either nervous or angry, though she had no idea how she knew that. Still, when her father or brothers were upset, she fed them. It kept her out of their way and gave her something to do. Plus, they always seemed to like what she whipped up. With limited supplies and no clue what this man liked to eat, she was definitely at a disadvantage, but cooking was her thing. Her joy. And her gut told her a meal would help Levi relax.

She was elbow deep in the freezer, digging out clearly labeled packages of meat and bags of frozen vegetables, when Levi came back into the kitchen. He was growling low, pacing. A wild animal trapped in an immaculate kitchen. Yet, oddly, he fit.

She wanted to fit with him. "Are you hungry?"

He stopped, watching her, looking almost wary. And a little…lustful. "I'm always hungry."

Amy shrugged, hiding her warming face by turning back to the freezer. "Then I'll cook."

"I don't know what kind of food is here."

"I do." She pulled a package of steaks out with a grin. "Now this, I can work with."

And she did.

Levi stayed close the entire time she worked in the kitchen. First sitting on the opposite side of the island, then slowly moving into her space. He helped her find pans and open a can of green beans, brushed past her on his way to the sink and the freezer. He growled and sniffed and kept looking out the windows, but he was *there*. Present in the moment.

Most of his attention was on her, the rest on keeping them safe. He cut an imposing silhouette against the dark cabinets, but she wasn't afraid. It felt right to be together. Alone. She could see this growing, see future dinners with this man. See a future, period.

As she cooked, she chatted about the restaurant and her life in town, about food and cooking and just about anything to fill the silence. Not that it was awkward to stop talking, just that there was so much she wanted him to know about her. And he listened, asked questions, kept the words flowing even though he said little about himself.

Levi left the room at one point, saying he needed to *sweep the perimeter*, whatever that meant. Amy was too focused on grating the hard cheese she'd found in the freezer. Cheese could cure most of what ailed you in her world. Cheese and wine… Damn, what she wouldn't give for a good bottle of red to serve with the meal.

When Levi snuck back into the kitchen, he crept up behind her. His warm breath on her shoulder and quiet growl nearly made her gasp. She ignored him, though, ignored the closeness. Focusing instead on mixing the cheese she'd grated and spices from one of the cabinets into the potato wedges she'd found in the freezer.

"I usually just warm those up," Levi murmured, his heated breath teasing her neck.

Amy shrugged off her shiver, her stomach tight with nerves. "You're protecting me. You deserve more than warmed-up potatoes."

He chuckled, leaning in to whisper a soft *thank you* before moving away once more. She tried to breathe normally, to stop shaking and control her body's reactions to him, but it took effort. As did ignoring the elephant in the room.

Neither of them was saying what needed to be said.

Both avoided the subject of mates, but not in a bad way. More in a teasing way, as if they were purposely building the anticipation. There was no denying the connection. If he felt the building mating imperative even half as strongly as she did, he'd have to be aware. Aware and quietly hunting, if she had to guess. That man was a force of nature, something wild that she wanted to chase and catch. Something she knew would make her just as wild if she let him. And she wanted to let him.

Less than an hour later, the steaks were defrosted and broiled to perfection, frozen potatoes were cooked, mashed, and cooked again, and green beans with garlic completed the meal. It may not have been perfect or from the freshest ingredients, but it was pretty and balanced. And she did know how to cook a steak, no matter what state it was in when she found it.

"This smells good." Levi sat back as she placed a plate in front of his spot at the counter. His smile lit something inside of her, making her almost blush for about the fifth time since she met him. Lord, she hadn't blushed since her preteen days. How he brought that out of her, she had no idea.

But she liked it. Hell, she loved it. "It'll taste even better."

"Of that, I have no doubt." He pulled out her chair, shooting her a cocky smile that made her heart trip. "Ladies first."

"Why, thank you." Once seated, she placed her napkin in her lap and smiled up at him. He was so close, so in her space, she couldn't hold back the words she'd been wanting to say. "I'm really glad we're here…together."

He stared, silent and still. Blinded, perhaps. Or surprised. Amy couldn't decipher the expression, but she definitely liked it.

Liked it even more when he whispered, "You're so pretty."

His soft voice brushed against her, and her breath caught. Before she could respond, he took his own seat. He even scooted his chair to be closer to her.

"This food really looks…good. It looks really good." He grabbed his water glass and brought it to his lips. His full, plump lips.

"You, too." Amy did blush this time if the heat rising to her ears was any indication. His eyebrows jumped as he grinned around the edge of the glass. "I mean, try it before you compliment me. The lack of fresh ingredients left me a little bit handcuffed."

He choked on his water, coughing harshly. Amy jumped and patted him on the back.

"Are you okay?"

"Fine," he said, even though he didn't sound fine.

Amy moved to slide off her seat. "Are you sure? I could get you—"

His warm hand came down on her thigh, not high enough to be a come-on, but definitely not the friendly arm pat she would have expected.

"I'm fine." He held her gaze as she retook her seat. "You just surprised me was all."

Amy thought back over her words, trying to determine what could have surprised him. She had just been talking about the food…and handcuffs. *Oh.*

"Oh." Her entire body went warm at the thought of being tied up…or down…by Levi. That particular act wasn't something she'd tried, but she wasn't against it. Hell, with Levi in her bed, she doubted she'd be against much of anything.

His hand left her thigh, his eyes looking anywhere but

at her. "Sorry," he whispered, sounding chastised. Almost…
ashamed.

Well, hell, that wouldn't do. "Don't be sorry, just don't
fall over dead before we've gotten the chance to try the
handcuffs. It'll be a new one for me."

He sputtered again, spinning to face her. If his eyes had
been any wider, he might have looked more like an owl than
a man. A strong, muscular, handsome man.

"What?" she asked with a casual shrug. "I understand
innuendo."

"You're dangerous." He blew out a breath, chuckling
softly. "Completely dangerous. It's not often someone
surprises me the way you have."

"Stick around, Leviathan. I'm pretty damn surprising."

His smile grew, lighting up his face. "I just might have
to do that."

Amy bit back a grin as they both cut into their steaks.
Just might have to indeed.

Thirteen

evi was in a hell of his own making. There was one bed on the first floor of the entire cabin. One very big, very soft, very comfortable bed that his mate was about to crawl into. Alone.

Fuck my life.

"Where will you sleep?" Amy sounded so shy, scared almost. It ate at something inside of him. Brought out his… less gentlemanly side. Threw him between the choices of stepping away to make her more comfortable and tossing her in the middle of that bad and *not* stepping away.

"I won't." Which could have meant a few different things, but right then, he needed to answer her question.

Her eyes were wide when they met his, her cheeks dark. Was she breathing heavy? "Why not?"

He couldn't resist her. Not like this, not in this room. Together. With that huge fucking bed right behind her. He ran a finger down the side of her face, slowly…giving her every chance to pull away. So fucking thankful when she leaned in to his touch instead. "I'll be on patrol, so being able to move around the house is better than being asleep."

"Oh." She stood silent, staring at her feet for a long moment as Levi's hand floated near her shoulder. He wanted to touch her again, to feel her skin against his, but he couldn't. If he did…he glanced at the bed again. Yeah. He couldn't touch her.

But Amy wasn't exactly one to wait for something she wanted, it seemed. She pounced, practically jumping into his arms. Wrapping her soft curves around his body and breathing into his neck. His growl was unstoppable, the way his hands slipped down to her ass something he couldn't control. Jesus, she was just so fucking *soft* all over.

"Thank you," she whispered, sounding so very scared. And didn't that just make him feel like an ass for grabbing her…well, ass. He brought his hands up to her waist, then higher to encircle her back. Squeezing her tight. He hadn't been hugged in a long time, would have said never except Bez's mate was a hugger. His memory included exactly three hugs—all from Sariel within the last year. But Amy's hug was bigger, bolder, so much more physical than his previous ones. She hugged with her entire body. She hugged him like she never wanted to let go.

He never wanted her to let go.

"Get some rest," he whispered, closing his eyes and giving her one final squeeze. "You're safe here with me."

"I know." She pulled away, biting her lip. Fuck, he was going to have the worst case of blue balls if she kept doing things like that.

Not yet, not yet, not yet.

Levi pulled himself together and took a single step away from her. A painful step. "The bathroom's through that door.

Yell if you need me."

"What constitutes need?" Amy cocked her head, looking adorably…naughty.

His growl slipped out before he could catch it, but he coughed it back. If he let his wolf take control, he'd never walk out of that room. Still… She did ask.

"Whatever you think does."

Her smile turned wicked, but she didn't pursue him. Instead, she grabbed her bag and tossed it over her shoulder. "Good to know."

With that, she disappeared into the bathroom, and Levi limped his way back to the living room, rubbing his aching cock through his jeans. He should have made her sleep in one of the bedrooms upstairs, but he hadn't wanted her that far away from him. It had seemed like a good decision, but at that particular moment, he wasn't so sure. What the hell was he going to do? He needed a little relief, but he couldn't risk her coming out of the bedroom and finding him with his hand in his jeans. Even though that visual had the possibility of an awesome ending. Maybe. Depended on what she did at that point, but his imagination was awesome, which didn't help his situation.

He took a few deep breaths and paced the room, trying to settle his mating instincts. He needed a distraction from her smell, her skin, her soft curves. Her ass. The sweep of it under her clothes. The plushness of it as it filled his hands. The way it—

One more press to his neglected cock and he grabbed his phone. Mammon. He needed to text Mammon and find out what was happening with Amy's pack. That was his need. Not jerking off to thoughts of Amy's ripe, round ass bouncing on his—

Must stop thinking about that ass.

He texted Mammon with a simple message.

What's doing?

Mammon hit him back almost immediately, giving Levi's thoughts no time to stray to the creature behind the bedroom door.

We've tracked the window perv to a house in town. Rental. Waiting on tenant details to move forward.

And the pack?

Thaus is on it.

Jesus, Thaus was involved. Even Abel would look like a pup next to their biggest Dire, not to mention, he made everyone around him seem like a fucking kid from the *Brady Bunch* in terms of personality. He would *not* fit in around the pack. Though, to be honest, it could be worse. They could have called on Dire Luc. No one compared to that man in terms of presence. That Dire oozed bad juju. But Levi couldn't get bogged down in the what-ifs of his team and Amy's family interacting. Mammon was a good choice to help the pack, and Thaus would be fine so long as he didn't scare the small children.

He was totally going to scare the small children.

Let me know what you and T find out.

Affirmative.

Levi tossed his phone on the table and plopped into the armchair with a sigh. Head back, legs spread, he focused inward. He needed to find his calm, to find his inner soldier and yank the fucker in front of the horny bastard who'd taken control of his mind. His mate was fragile right now, tossed into this situation with him with no warning. She was probably scared half out of her wits. He couldn't just rut her through the floor like an animal.

But someday, he was going to rut her through the floor like an animal. And he was going to make sure she liked it as much, if not more, than he did.

That thought brought his hand back to his cock. He could feel the wetness at the tip, the precome collecting there. There was no way this was disappearing without a little hands-on attention. He could jack off out here, but there was the chance Amy would catch him. Plus, he never was the biggest fan of the old lotion-and-tissue job. He was a shower jerker, and there was a perfectly good shower twenty feet away behind a locking door.

He slid his hands inside his pants, sighing as skin met skin. Give her a few minutes…make sure she had time to fall asleep. Then he could sneak in and take a shower. She wouldn't think anything weird about that, right? A man had to shower.

He hissed as he stroked himself, the pleasure-pain of it sending tingles shooting down his legs. Images of his mate joining him bombarded his brain, making him growl softly and stroke harder. On her back, on her knees, on all fours… she'd be beautiful in any position. Be sexy as hell, too. He wanted her every way. Wanted her under him, on top of him, riding his face. Didn't matter. He wanted all sorts of things he figured she wasn't ready for. Hopefully, she would be…someday.

As his fingers pulled back his foreskin on a rough jerk, he hissed and bucked, knowing his hand might be all he'd be getting for some time and not giving a damn. She was worth it. He'd waited this long for her—he could wait years more if he had to. Could wait another lifetime for her to come around and accept him.

His leg shook with his need to come. Close…he was so close already. Fuck time to let her fall asleep. If she was still awake, he'd just tell her he needed a shower. She didn't have to know what was going on. He was a grown man, for fuck's sake. He could hide a hard-on.

Standing, he tucked himself back inside his pants and zipped up. Adjusted a time or two, just to be sure. He tiptoed through the living room and to the bedroom door, trying to stay silent on the old wood floors. There was no sound from behind the door, no rustle of fabric. Only her heartbeat and the even whisper of her breaths. Hopefully, she was already asleep.

Holding his breath, Levi crept inside. The moonlight streaming through the windows lit the room enough for him to see Amy curled up in the middle of that big bed. Fuck, she was beautiful. And if he didn't get himself into the shower, he was going to come just looking at her.

He edged around the foot of the bed, his eyes stuck on his mate. That really was his downfall. He was too busy staring at her to see the bag against the footboard. Too distracted to watch where he was going.

Which was why he tripped.

Cursing as he fell, he slammed a hand onto the footboard to keep from going down face first. Amy jumped up, staring at him, her thin tank top giving everything underneath it away. He gripped the footboard harder, hanging on, hoping like hell he was strong enough to stay in place and not just pounce on her.

"What's wrong?" Her voice made him want to moan, made his cock jerk in his jeans.

"Nothing." He licked his lips, his mouth so dry he could barely speak. "I tripped."

She looked around the room and cocked her head. She wasn't dumb enough not to notice the brightness of the moonlight. "How did you trip?"

"I was distracted." Which wasn't a lie. He was still distracted. It took physical effort to keep his eyes on hers and not stare at all that was exposed to him. God, what had he done to deserve such bad fucking karma? His mate…almost naked…in this bed…and he couldn't touch.

Amy, meanwhile, seemed determined to make his living hell that much worse. "Distracted? By what?"

And wasn't that the question of the hour? Levi had two choices…lie, or tell the truth. And being that this was his mate he was talking to, the woman the fates deemed his perfect match, there was only one right answer.

"By you." Levi closed his eyes and took a deep breath, giving in. "By my beautiful mate lying in this ridiculously huge bed. All alone. That's what distracted me."

"Oh, thank fuck." She sighed and sat back, letting the blanket slip even more. Exposing more of her skin to him and pulling the tank top a bit tighter. Fuck, her nipples were hard.

"Levi."

He jerked, tearing his eyes away from her breasts. "What?"

Amy smiled all slow and sly. "You've been avoiding the mate word this whole time. I was wondering when we'd get to that."

Her words scrambled his brain, brought his full attention right back to her. Except for the bit still focused on his cock. "You haven't exactly been screaming it from the rooftops."

"I was waiting for you." And she shrugged. As if it was nothing. As if the thin fabric covering her didn't drag across her erect nipples with that little move. Why was she trying to kill him?

He took a deep breath and stood, angling his body so she wouldn't see how hard he was for her. Still. "I didn't want to overwhelm you. You have a lot going on."

She leaned back, tugged the comforter until one leg

peeked out. One long, bare leg. Very bare. All the way up bare. Jesus, this girl was playing a dangerous game and she had no idea. He was gasoline ready to explode, ready for the slightest spark to start the flames.

And then she lit a match.

"Maybe I want to be overwhelmed."

Fourteen

Amy's entire body burned with the heat of her need. Every inch, every bit. Just the fact that her mate was right there at the foot of the bed made her body throb with the need to be closer. Deep down, she knew the overwhelming desire flooding her was nothing more than the mating imperative. The body's way of reminding two newly mated shifters that their bond needed to be sealed. She knew it, but she didn't care. They were alone, safe, together…and she *wanted*.

She slid her foot up the mattress, bending her knee, letting the blanket fall farther so he could see more of her. See the tiny panties she wore with her tank top. See that there was nothing else on her body. He growled in response, his fingers practically cracking the footboard. That growl, those knuckles going pale with the strength of his grip… He was holding himself back, and that just wouldn't do.

"Levi." She sighed and fell back against the pillows, pulling the blanket tight between her legs. Teasing herself with the drag of the fabric against her flesh. "Don't you feel it?"

"What, doll?" His gravelly voice fanned the flames, burning her from the inside out. "Tell me what you feel?"

"Hot. Bothered." She slid a hand between her legs, letting her fingers trail over the cotton there. "Needy."

"Shit," he hissed, his rumble growing louder. Rougher. Deeper.

The sound pulled Amy's growl from her. Her wolf peeked through her human eyes, sneaking an investigatory look at her fated mate. Watching him resist the temptation laid before him. The beast liked what she saw. His muscles enticed her as the flesh of someone fit and strong, someone protective. Someone solid and worthy. Amy's wolf approved of her mate. Which was a good thing, because Amy was about to implode with the need to be claimed by him.

"This bed is too big for me." Amy bit her bottom lip, spreading her knees farther apart. "Join me."

"I...can't."

Amy groaned, slipping her fingers under the fabric between her legs. Teasing herself skin on skin. "Why not?"

Levi's fist clutched the wood harder, his knuckles practically glowing in the moonlight, the clawed tips of his fingers embedded in the hardwood. "If I take one step closer, I won't be able to be a gentleman."

"Maybe I don't want you to be."

"Amy, I mean it. You have no idea what I want to do to you."

That got her attention.

"What do you want to do? Tell me." She kept her fingers playing between her legs and her eyes on her mate. Watching as he fought with his control. Daring him to break. "Please."

It had to be the please that shattered Levi's resistance.

Or maybe it was the wet sound of her fingers sliding inside herself. Amy may never know, not that it mattered. All she cared about was the way his eyes seemed to devour her, the way his entire body leaned toward her. The way he responded to what she offered.

His growl—that deep, luscious sound that made her positively drip for him—turned to a snarl before he cut the rumble off completely. "I want to strip you down and lick every inch of you. I want to crawl up your body and feel your skin rub against mine." He leaned forward, one hand on the mattress, still holding on to the footboard with the other. "I want to tease you with my fingers and tongue until I have you bucking and begging and clenching, then slide inside you and fuck you until you can't see. Until I make you come so hard, I can feel you pulling my cock deeper. Until I make that beautiful pussy mine."

Amy arched her back as she pushed her fingers deeper. The blankets fell completely to the side, baring her body to him, letting him see exactly what his words did to her. He growled at the sight, hissing a curse that had her clenching already.

"Oh," she groaned, wishing so hard for him to replace her hand. To take over. To give her what she so desperately needed. "Levi, please."

Levi grabbed Amy's ankle and yanked her down the bed, spreading her before him. She yelped, pulling her hand from between her legs to grasp at the comforter beneath her. His hungry eyes met hers, nearly pure silver already. Looking so otherworldly. A whisper of a memory flitted through Amy's head, something told to her as a child, a legend about wolves with silver eyes, but it disappeared into the ether as Levi licked his bottom lip and finally released that damn footboard. He brought one hand to her inner thigh, gripping her, pushing her leg down and teasing the flesh leading to where she wanted him most. Where she needed him. Her entire body clamped down with that one touch, sending a shiver up her spine that had her eyes rolling back.

"Oh, God." She gasped and arched, craving more. Wanting to feel that spark again.

"God can't help you now." He crawled over top of her, pushing up the tiny tank top along the way. "You're mine."

"Yes." Amy arched into his touch, so needy for him, so desperate. "Please, Levi."

"I like it when you beg." His lips closed around her nipple, sucking and pulling with a pressure that made her shake. A tug at Amy's hip was the only warning she received before her panties disappeared. Victims of his claws and strength. The very thought of it, the idea of him literally tearing away the barriers between them, was enough to bring her right to that edge. Amy's body clenched, needing something, wanting so desperately to be filled. To be stretched. To be worked over.

Hands in his hair, pulling him up her body, Amy arched and kicked, wanting his pants off. Needing him naked against her. Craving the heat of his skin, the weight of him upon her. Levi must have understood those desires. Without releasing her nipple from his attack, he slid a hand between the two of them to unfasten his jeans. Teasing her with the backs of his fingers. Amy released a deep rumble of a growl and brought her legs up, hooking her toes into the waistband of his pants and pushing them down his legs. Kicking them as far as she could before she was stretched underneath him.

"Please," she whispered, wrapping one leg around his hip to pull him against her. "Want you."

"Got me." He bit her nipple, bringing his hands under her shoulders to pull her tighter. "You've got every inch of me, doll."

Irritated by the fabric against her skin, Amy pulled her tank top the rest of the way off. Finally, nothing but skin between them. Nothing but his heat mixing with hers. She rocked her hips in time with him, loving the pressure the move gave her. The tingles each rub sent shooting up her spine. She was so ready, so needy and wanton. So over the waiting.

"Now, Levi," she groaned, clawing his shoulders. "Make me come."

Without a bit of warning, he thrust inside her. Amy bit back a scream as he pushed deep inside, as he took want he wanted. What she had offered up so willingly. She moaned and gripped him tighter, staring up at him, losing herself in those swirling silver eyes.

He moved with an intention and control Amy had never experienced, stroking deep, keeping a hold on her shoulders to use as leverage. Pinning her down in a way that screamed dominance. His entire body undulated against her, waves of muscles contracting to pull himself deeper. To press on all the parts that would drive her wild. To keep her right on that edge of her release.

"Fuck, you're so soft and wet." His eyes fluttered nearly closed as he groaned and pressed deeper. "I want to feel you come on my cock, doll. Want to make you scream."

Amy moaned, nibbling along his neck as she wrapped her legs around his hips. He was so deep already, so wide and almost punishing. Blunt, she would have said in a moment when he wasn't making her brain scramble. But that bluntness felt amazing; the almost painful way he filled her so damn delicious. Especially when he pressed deep and rotated his hips, giving her clit a solid rub with the base of him. Yeah. That felt good. Really good.

Without so much as a hint, Levi pulled out of her,

leaving her confused and desperate for about half a second. He grabbed her leg and flipped her onto her stomach, leaving her gasping and tense as she waited to see what would happen next. Not that he made her wait long.

Levi pressed himself on top of her again, this time pushing her into the mattress. The weight of him stifled her movements, controlled her, held her in place. With barely a breath between moves, Levi spread her legs with his knees and pushed back inside her from behind. Pressing deep without breaking his rhythm. Amy whimpered as she clutched at the sheets.

"Do you know why I want you like this?" His whispered growl against her neck made her shiver, and she shook her head. His hand slipped beneath them, fingers finding her throbbing clit. Rubbing it. Making her tense up at the coming onslaught of sensation.

But that shake wasn't enough for him apparently. Levi smacked her ass, harder than a tap but not painful. A delicious shock to her system that elicited a yelp from her. "Are you going to answer me, doll?"

"No. I mean…I don't know." She gasped and shook, trying to concentrate on him but lost to her pleasure. To the way her muscles were already clenching in preparation of what she knew was to come. To the feel of him pressing her into the mattress and holding her down. "Please, Levi."

He bit her shoulder, harder than a nibble but not enough to break the skin. Fuck, she wanted him to break it, though. Wanted him to claim her. To sink his teeth as deep as his dick and own every inch of her.

He chuckled, sliding his fingers along either side of her clit in a deliciously teasing stroke. "I want you like this because you're so expressive. Everything I did to you, every ounce of pleasure I gave you, was written right on that gorgeous face. You made me so desperate to come, my doll. Too desperate."

He grew a bit rougher, his hips snapping against hers and his hand stilling. Not that it needed to move. The simple act of him fucking her, rocking her back and forth, was enough to keep his fingers in contact with her clit.

Amy writhed beneath him, trying to get that last push, that last little hint of sensation that would throw her over the edge. Would start the rush of pleasure she frantically needed. But his weight kept her still, his hips forcing her body to move as he wanted it to. She was completely at his mercy, and he wasn't ready to let her go yet.

"I want to fuck you for days." He growled and shifted his angle, hitting new depths inside of her that made her bury her face in the pillow to hide her scream. "I want to feel you come on my cock, my fingers, and my tongue just so I know I've given you as much pleasure as watching you gives me. Want to learn every move to entice you so I can please you, so I can get you to make those gaspy moans again and again. But I couldn't watch anymore. Fuck, doll. You're living, breathing desire, and I'll never be able to compete. I don't even want to… I just want to hear you scream your pleasure." He thrust faster, curling his fingers to give her more.

"Fuck, Levi." Amy sighed, trying so hard to move, to touch, to grab at something. Anything. "You're going to make me come if you keep that up."

He chuckled, a dirty sound that sent a shiver shooting up her spine. "You make me want to come just by walking in the room."

Levi pinched her clit hard, and Amy fell. Clenching, crying his name, squeezing him as her body locked down and rode out the pleasure. Levi thrust faster and harder, pushing into her with a strength that overwhelmed her, sliding her up the mattress with the fierceness of the way he fucked her. The way he took what he needed.

One last push and he came, roaring his release before bringing his mouth back to her shoulder. Holding her down with his teeth pressing against her neck. Teasing her with the feel of what they both wanted.

"Please," she begged, angling her head to give him room. "Please give me your bite. I want it. I need it."

Levi growled, his hips still jerking into hers, his body still weighting her down. "Not yet. Not the first time. I want to make this last. Want to feel you come a hundred times first."

She gasped as his teeth dug a little deeper, as a shot of pain—quick and slight—rushed through her.

"But soon. I promise you." He licked the back of her neck, the slow rumble of his growl teasing her sweat-soaked skin. "Very, very soon."

Fifteen

Levi awoke to a predawn glow lighting the bedroom in an ethereal sort of way…and a hard-on the likes of which he'd never experienced. He positively ached for his mate. Lucky thing she was right beside him. Well, beside wasn't quite the right descriptor. In his sleep, he'd ended up with his lips against Amy's neck and his hand between her legs. And he wasn't just pressed against her; he was practically on top of her. He could use the excuse that his wolf was probably protecting her while they slept, but he doubted the truth would be so altruistic. His hard-as-steel cock nestled snugly against her ass was proof of that.

Plus the fact that he'd woken up three times overnight in the exact same position.

And still, as he pushed off the haze of a solid few hours' sleep, he crept closer. It was as if his body couldn't get close enough, even in his sleep. As if his subconscious sought out her soft curves and hidden secrets. Well, not so secret after last night. He knew exactly how tight that pussy was, how warm and soft. And how wet…still. Every time he'd woken overnight, he'd ended up buried inside her, made her come too many times to count. But he wasn't done. Not yet. Not by a long shot.

He rocked his hand back and forth, letting his thumb tease her opening. Fuck, she was so wet already. All the things he should do—patrol the house again, monitor the perimeter of the property now that it was daylight, check in with his brothers as he'd failed to do all night—were mere whispers in his mind. They should have been demands, should have had his soldier training kicking in to override his libido. But they weren't…at all. He had his warm, snuggly mate in his arms. Had the taste of her skin on his tongue, her plump ass practically hugging his needy cock, and her arousal on his fingers. He wasn't moving from this spot.

Well, he was definitely moving, just not to leave the bed. Not yet.

He let his fingers explore through her tight curls as he slid his lips and teeth back and forth across her shoulder. Teasing her, preparing her for what he had planned. The mission he was mounting. Amy sighed and moved with him on instinct alone it seemed, spreading her legs and rocking her hips. It wasn't until he had his fingers deep inside her and his cock rutting against her ass that she woke up, though.

"Levi," she moaned, dragging his name out in a way that made his beast growl in pure sensual delight. Fuck, that was hot.

"Say it again." He pushed his fingers deeper, keeping the heel of his hand against her clit. Keeping her on edge. "Say my name just like that."

She rocked into him, her growl matching his. Her entire body shivering as she neared her climax. "Levi."

Yep. That was it. He rolled her forward, using his body weight to trap her underneath him. He liked her like this—facedown, under his control, and almost helpless to seek her own pleasure. She could try, could wriggle and writhe beneath his weight, but there was nothing to rub against. Nothing to push her closer. Every sigh, every shiver, every single beat of her heart as she chased her orgasm was on him. Leading her to the edge of her resistance, watching her shatter, feeling her positively drip because of the things he'd done—now, *that* was satisfying. He'd get her there again, just like last night. Better than last night. He had to.

Fingers deep and hand teasing, Levi opened his mouth over the muscle leading from her neck to her shoulder and touched his teeth to her skin. Grabbed her with them. It was a wolf sort of warning, a call to the animal within her to settle. To let him lead. To submit.

Amy gasped, her shiver turning into a full-body shake. Her pussy clenched around his fingers, walls fluttering in a way that told him how close she was. Already. He had to get inside her before he missed his chance. Had to hold her down and fuck her until she cried his name in that breathy tone a thousand times. Had to go balls deep and show her who owned that warm, wet pussy he had in his hand.

So he did.

Dragging his hand from her heaven, he lined himself up and thrust. One push. No soft nudges or slow movements. His girl liked it hard and fast and rough. At least, she had last night, and he was fucking thankful for that.

His pace left no room for talking, though she tried. Little gasps of his name as he slid deep, mewls and cries as he made sure her clit got the attention it deserved. But the best was the way she would growl and snarl when his teeth pressed into her shoulder. Soon… That claiming bite would come soon. But not yet. Not until they talked about everything. Until she knew what his life was like and could decide if she wanted to be with him forever. A mating bite was a one-shot deal, no take-backs, no returns. She needed to be sure before he claimed her that way. Even he wasn't that much of an animal.

Still, he rutted against her until she had to place both hands against the headboard to keep from sliding into it. And Levi took advantage of that position, wrapping himself around her and holding on tight. One arm around her chest with his hand on her tit, one around her hips with his fingers flicking that pretty clit. He owned her body with every stroke, every shift, every fucking pinch and rub. Fucked her hard and deep until she came with his name falling from her lips. Until he emptied inside of her with a grunt and a harsher bite to her neck. Until they were once again sweaty and sated…for the moment.

"Well, good morning," she said with a laugh as she finally rolled over to face him. Her eyes were bright, her hair completely wild, and her face was flushed. She had a bruise on her neck from his teeth, a mark that made Levi's wolf go wild. She was the most beautiful thing he'd ever seen, and she was his.

But he couldn't keep his eyes off that mark. "Good morning to you, mate."

She growled and wrapped herself around him. Pulled him in for a deep, wet kiss that ended far too soon. "I like the sound of that."

His hands were unstoppable, running up and down her body. Following every soft curve. Exploring every dip. His eyes still going back to that oval mark that made him want to purr in pleasure. But reality had begun to sneak into his thoughts, things like responsibilities and missions. Things that should have taken precedence.

He hated the words he needed to say next. "I should get up."

"Why?" She bent her leg, rubbing her thigh against where he was growing hard for her again.

Levi leaned down and kissed her nose. A silly act even as his hand slid between her legs to tease her some more. "Need to check the house."

Amy moaned and spread her legs wider. An invitation Levi couldn't resist. He plunged inside, curling his fingers to find that sweet spot. She was so wet, so swollen still. The picture of sweet debauchery in his bed. Him practically on top of her, naked skin glistening in the low light, legs spread and pussy so wet and wanting. Perfect…every fucking inch.

As Levi twisted his hand to press his thumb alongside her clit, Amy groaned again and clutched at his shoulders. Bucking her hips and trying to pull him closer.

"The house is fine. Great. Perfect," she said, as her wild eyes met his. Desiring eyes…filled with a need that broke every bit of will he had left. As did her words.

"Fuck, come inside me again. Please."

Levi growled and surrendered, though not completely. There were things to do to keep her safe, but he could give her one more orgasm before he pulled himself away. He just needed to be thorough. So he did as she wanted—sort of— plunging three of his fingers deep inside her. Focusing on the feel of her skin, the sound of her harsh breathing, and ignoring the procedures and tactics racing through his brain.

Amy groaned with every move of his hand, so fucking responsive to his touch. That knowledge made his dick practically weep for her. He nuzzled her neck as his fingers stroked and plunged and drove his mate wild, licking and nibbled where he wanted to bite. Where he wanted to claim her.

"Want it," Amy gasped, tilting her head back to give him more room. "Please."

His growl became something long and unbreakable, a constant rumbling through the room. "You don't know—"

She grabbed his hand, stopping him, his fingers trapped inside her pussy. "Don't assume I'm some weak-minded girl who doesn't know what I'm getting myself into. You're my mate and I'm yours. It's a forever connection. Yes, there's danger around us, but you've already promised to keep me safe. We'll learn about each other as we go…trial by fire." She let go of his hand, rocking her hips so he would finger her again, nuzzling his neck up to his ear. "I trust you. I want you. Bite me, Leviathan. I want to feel you inside of me in all ways. Please, my mate."

He couldn't have resisted that please for anything. She didn't know yet, hadn't been told about his heritage. About the secret he held or the lifestyle he lived because of his wolf. But she wanted *him*, the man, and he'd give that to her. She'd learn about the Dire Wolf eventually.

"As you wish." He pulled his hand from between her legs and once again pressed his cock inside. She was swollen with her arousal, tighter than before, and that made it so much harder to hold back. He wanted her close when he bit. Wanted her begging for something. For him.

Legs around his waist, eyes staring into his, Amy smiled and enticed him. Worked her sorcery over him until there was nothing in the world but the two of them and that moment. Just sex and care and heartstrings tied together forever.

And teeth. Then there were teeth.

His canines descended as he ran them along her neck, bursting through the gums and giving her a feel of what was to come. Giving her an out. One more minute. That's all he needed. One more minute of fucking his mate, and he'd be ready to come. Ready to give as he took. Ready for whatever this moment led to.

He ground deep, keeping an eye on the way she arched into him, how she gasped and shivered. On the way her eyes closed and her head tilted back with every thrust. She was so beautiful like this, and she was close. Almost there. Right on the edge of—

"Levi, now."

She came with a moan that put his beast completely in control, and Levi bit down with purpose. The orgasm that hit him had to be as strong if not stronger than the one she was having, the one milking his cock with every clench. Fuck, he was right at the edge with her—somewhere between best orgasm ever and fearful she'd squeeze hard enough to break him. And still, he kept going, kept rocking into her, kept biting and sucking and taking. He took in her essence and gave her his before licking the wound and rolling them over. Offering himself to her the only way he knew how, by letting her lead. Subjugating himself.

And she took that dominion with a growl and a grin down at him as she rode through her orgasm. She leaned down, nuzzling his face before heading right for his neck. He tilted his head, ready, needing to feel the sting of her bite as he'd needed to give her his. Thank the fates she didn't make him wait.

Her teeth entered his skin, and he died with her name on his lips. Not literally, but it certainly felt as if his life was over. Dead and brought back to start anew, to begin all over with only her. His cock jerked and throbbed, another orgasm rocking his body all the way to his toes as she gave back what he'd already taken from her. He felt her pleasure mixed with his own, felt the spirit of her in ways he'd never experienced.

He felt *her*, and it was amazing.

— —

Too many hours of continually fucking his mate was as long as Levi could ignore the need to protect her. Already, his wolf was pacing in his mind, needing to monitor and patrol. Wanting to reach out to his pack. Fuck, but the mating haze was hard to pull away from.

"Why don't you shower?" Levi licked her neck, eyeing his claiming bite. Growing hard again just by seeing it on her skin. He was going to need to stock up on electrolytes and energy shots if his mating drive kept up at this pace.

"Why don't you come with me?" She ran her fingers over his arm, teasing him. Again. He'd have to get one of his brothers to bring supplies—there was no way he was going to a store without her, and if he took her with him, they'd probably end up having sex in an aisle.

Sadly, he needed to focus on something other than sex for a minute.

Levi growled and held her to him for one more sweet moment before rolling away. "Because if I join you, I'll fuck you against the tiles until the water runs cold."

"Not seeing the problem there."

He chuckled, rubbing circles on his chest above where his heart beat for the woman by his side. "I need to do a perimeter inspection and check in with my brothers. Otherwise, yes, I'd happily follow you into that stone shower and show you what I can do to you while standing up."

Amy chuckled before rolling out of bed. "Fine. Send me off to get clean without you."

Levi growled and rolled with her, almost whimpering when she actually left the bed. She was naked, gloriously, totally naked, and wasn't shy about walking around like that. Not that he expected her to be. Her entire body was on display for him, every scratch and red spot from their sex-filled night. Every centimeter of that claiming bite practically glowing.

"You are so fucking beautiful."

The words were soft and unplanned, but that apparently didn't matter to Amy. She grinned and bent over him, giving him one last taste of her lips.

"And you are so fucking amazing, mate."

He growled and kissed her one last time before lying back. "Go. Before I pull you on top of me and let you ride me again."

"Still not seeing the problem there."

Levi sighed as she walked into the bathroom and closed the door behind her. Yeah, there was a problem. The problem being someone peeking at his mate and getting too close to her pack. The problem being the fact that they were on the run, not tucked away for some kind of mating honeymoon. He had a job to do here, and his dick needed to stand down for a few hours so he could make sure she was safe. But good goddamn, he was totally going to have her ride him next time. Just the thought of those tits swinging as she took her pleasure from him had his dick standing up and begging.

Later…definitely later.

He yanked on a pair of jeans and stalked through the house, checking every window and door. Sniffing as he passed through the rooms. The whole place smelled like him and Amy and sex, which pleased his territorial inner wolf. But it made the man uncomfortable. The scent was so strong, so permeated through the space, he could barely smell anything beyond it. Someone could be hiding on the porch, and he wasn't sure he'd know. A dangerous thought.

His mate and danger did not need to be so close together.

When he finally made it back to the living room, he grabbed his phone from the table where he'd left it. Thirty alerts. All texts and, later, missed calls from his brothers. Every one a reminder of how he should have gotten out of bed hours ago.

Motherfucker.

Amy walked out of the bedroom as he was scrolling through the alerts. "What's wrong?"

He shook his head, his brow pulling down as words and names rolled past his eyes. "They know who's been watching you."

"Who?" She grabbed his arm, seeking security, looking up at him with an expression of trust and fear. That look gutted him. Shit, he needed to get his head together, needed to do his damn job so nothing happened to her. He needed to stop thinking with his dick.

Mammon would be proud of that decision…sort of.

"Some guy named Randall Johnson. Sound familiar?" When she shook her head, he typed out a quick message asking for pictures. "Get dressed. Shoes and all."

"Why?" But even as she asked, she moved. Grabbing her coat and sliding her feet into the winter boots she'd been wearing when they left her house the night before.

"If my guys haven't tracked him down yet, we need to get back on the road."

"But I thought we were safe here."

Her words hit him like a fist to the chest. "You're not safe until this guy is captured. If he's left town, he could sneak up on us. I don't want a confrontation here. This place isn't set up for a battle." He slipped an arm around her waist and pulled her closer. Leaning in to nuzzle her ear as he whispered, "You're my mate. You deserve the best in terms of safety. This place isn't the best. If he's still loose, we'll need more fortification."

She sighed and nodded, clinging to Levi's shoulders. "He's only human."

Levi kissed the top of her head, having thought the same thing before he knew this "only human" was after the one woman the fates deemed perfect for him. "I won't underestimate him just because of that."

Levi's phone sounded with two texts back to back. Thaus had shot him a *where the fuck have you been* message, but Mammon came through. His message contained a single image file of what looked like a mug shot.

He held it up for Amy to see. "Know him?"

Amy's brow came down as she looked, then she reached for the phone. "That's Gavin."

The spike of jealousy was hard to kick back. "Who's Gavin?"

Amy glanced at him then back at the phone. "Gavin Michelson. He's the new kindergarten teacher in town. He comes to the diner every day."

The snarl of his wolf broke the silence of the house. He snatched the phone back from her and sent a quick text back to the team.

Alias Gavin Michelson. Kindergarten teacher and patron of the diner.

"I served him coffee," Amy whispered, her face pale. Levi kept an arm around her, kept her pressed against him. She was too sweet to understand how manipulative and sneaky people could be, too innocent to have seen the worst side of mankind. He hated that she was learning those lessons at all, but at least she had him to guide her.

"Are you okay?" he asked, still clutching his phone.

"I just...I feel betrayed. Literally, every single day, I've served that man coffee. And he was…watching me."

"I know. But now we have intel. My brothers will track him down and take him into custody. We'll all keep you safe."

Still, even as the words left his lips, he knew they were just that…words.

"I'll grab you a shirt," Amy said, her voice too quiet, too soft. Distracted. She pulled out of his embrace and shuffled toward the bedroom with a slow step and a hanging head. Levi wanted to go after her, but he had a feeling she needed a moment to come to grips with the fact that someone she thought she knew was really a dangerous liar. That was never an easy fact to accept.

She was walking back to him, black T-shirt in hand, when his phone rang. His stomach bottomed out before he even swiped to answer. His team wouldn't call without reason.

"Yeah?"

Mammon's voice was deeper than normal. "Get out."

His eyes darted to the door, expecting a threat to come barreling through. "Situation?"

"Don't grab anything except the Omega. We know he followed you out of town, but we can't pinpoint exactly where he is at this moment."

Levi jumped into action without a word. He disconnected the call, grabbed Amy by the waist, and tossed her over his shoulder, running for the front door. A quick grab of his keys and he was outside, growling with every step as he raced toward the truck.

"Levi, what—"

He shushed her with a snarl, tossing her into the cab from the driver's side door. "Slide over."

She scooted as he hopped in, looking scared but

responding to his demands. "Please tell me what's going on."

Levi gunned the engine, throwing the beast into gear and spinning the tires on the loose gravel as he shot forward. "He's here."

The first gunshot sounded as she clicked her seat belt into place, the thunk of the bullet hitting the liftgate way too close for comfort.

"Hang on." He slammed his foot down on the gas pedal, heading for the road. No other car was in sight, no tail visible. He'd need to keep an eye out behind him, but it seemed as if the bastard was on foot. That gave Levi the advantage of speed. He just needed to haul ass so he could get far enough ahead of the guy.

Two dirt roads driven down way too fast, one nasty slide of a turn onto a small country highway, and about a thousand glances in the rearview mirror were enough to let the immediate panic he'd experienced begin to settle. But that opened him up for guilt to drown him in its sticky hold. This was his fault. He could have had her halfway to a better safe house already had he kept his dick to himself. Could have figured out hours earlier that the fucker was close had he just followed procedure.

"Stop it," Amy said, interrupting his mental flagellation.

"Stop what?"

"Stop beating yourself up. This isn't your fault."

He shook his head. "I should have kept my phone near me."

"And I should have known a man was watching me through my windows. I should have smelled him at the very least."

"None of this is your fault."

"It's not yours either, so stop berating yourself. I'm glad you found me, I'm glad you're my mate, and I'm really glad you fucked me halfway to death all night and this morning."

Levi sighed. "Amy—"

"Do you regret the sex?"

He wanted to look at her, to bear witness to her expression, but he was doing over a hundred miles an hour and couldn't take his eyes from the road for a single second. All he could do was answer her honestly.

"No."

"The claiming bites?"

He growled, unable to hold it back. His wolf was a possessive motherfucker. "Not at all."

"Then quit beating yourself up. The need to join with a new mate is hard to resist." She chuckled and flattened herself against the door, bringing her feet onto the seat between them. "Hell, I'd give you road head right now if there wasn't a guy with a gun behind us somewhere."

He grinned, shaking his head at his smartass mate. "Road head, huh? Don't think I'd turn that down, to be honest."

"Good to know." Her foot came to rest on his thigh. "Now drive faster. Guns freak me out."

He hit an on-ramp for an expressway heading south and spun the wheel, squealing and drifting into the curve before the tires caught traction.

"As you wish."

Sixteen

Amy had once thought exploring the country by car would be fascinating. Road trips had an appeal that her sheltered, restricted self found intriguing. There was a freedom in that fantasy, something she never had but always craved when she was growing up on her mountain. The open road, the hopping from place to place, the possibilities for exploring…all of it had sounded so fun and carefree.

She had been so very wrong. Living on the road, in constant motion, sucked ass.

Amy shifted in her seat, trying to find a comfortable spot that wouldn't put her looking right at the rising sun. But after two days in a truck, nothing was comfortable. Nothing at all. She smelled, she was tired, she was cranky, and her mate was too focused on outrunning the ghost chasing them to let them sit still for more than a few minutes. All that moving meant no sex, either. Which really shouldn't have been her priority, but being in such close quarters with

Levi—especially after just exchanging mating bites—wasn't easy on her in any way, shape, or form. Including the sexual way.

"You need to sleep," she mumbled as Levi yawned for about the millionth time since the sun had peeked over the horizon.

"I'm good."

Damn stubborn man. "You're not good; you're exhausted."

He paused, the silence filled only with the sound of the tires eating up pavement, and then he shook his head. "We can't stop."

Amy's sigh couldn't have been any bigger…it was physically impossible. "That's what you keep saying."

Levi growled a little, which didn't help the situation. How dare he get angry with her? This was *his* plan. What was she supposed to do…sit quietly and pretend everything was fine? Everything was not *fine*. It was so far past fine, she couldn't even imagine what fine was anymore.

But apparently, Levi didn't understand that, because he opened his mouth. "I know this isn't exactly a load of fun, but it's necessary. This guy slipped past my brothers, which means he's way more than just some average human. Plus, there were multiple scent trails in the mountains—until we know where he is and how many friends he's got with him, we keep moving. It's the only way I can figure to keep you completely safe while we're still in this fucking mating haze. If you can think up a plan to manage guarding you, patrolling wherever we stop, and not having sex on every available surface, flat or not, then offer it up. Otherwise, we stick with mine and stay on the road until my brothers give us a safe house to head for. And I could do without the attitude right now."

She closed her eyes, locking down the growl that was burning up her throat. Trying so hard to hold back her frustrations. Trying, and failing miserably.

"Attitude? This isn't attitude. This is me stuck in a truck with my mate who refuses to stop for more than the most cursory of reasons. I haven't used a non-gas station bathroom in days, haven't eaten real food in just as long, and my hips actually hurt from sitting on this damn bench seat. I'm a shifter, Leviathan. You almost fucking me through the mattress didn't make my hips hurt this bad. No part of me should hurt from anything so sedentary." Amy sighed, running a hand through her filthy hair. "I need a shower, a bed, and about twelve orgasms. Not necessarily in that order. So if you think this is attitude, please, keep driving in these crazy circles all over the place with no end in sight. Another day or so, and I'll show you exactly how much *attitude* you're mated to."

Levi sat rigid and silent, staring straight ahead. The air in the truck developed a weight, bearing down on her like a physical being. Even her wolf reacted to it, going still in her mind, big eyes watching for the first sign of threat. Amy worried he was going to crack and yell back at her, maybe tell her how selfish she was being. Because she was—she knew it—but that didn't mean she was ready to hear it. She hoped he could bite back any negative response, but tempers were funny things. Hers had been sprung, and though she felt better, she also worried. What if her mate didn't take well to her raising her voice? What if he got mad? What if—

His throaty chuckle interrupted her spiraling thoughts. She stared, unable to believe she was hearing what she thought she was, and growing more frustrated at his obvious dismissal of her feelings.

"Why are you laughing?"

He turned that grin on her, the one that made her insides quiver. The one she hadn't seen in days. "Because you're aiming so low, sweetheart."

"What do you mean, aiming low?"

He reached across the seat, his big hand landing on her thigh and squeezing in a possessive move that made her heart thump. God, if only his fingers were half an inch higher. She slouched into his hold almost on instinct, searching out the feel of him against her. Wishing for it.

"Not yet, doll." He slid his hand toward her knee with a shake of his head. "But yes, aiming low. Because if you think I'm going to stop at twelve orgasms for you once we eliminate the threat to you and your pack, you're totally underestimating my attention span. And my skills."

And there he was, her mate, back to being his teasing, sexy self. "Oh, really? You think you can handle that much, huh?"

He hummed and shook his head. "Your lack of faith is downright insulting."

For the first time in three days, she laughed. Truly, deeply guffawed right there in the cabin of the truck. Not caring that her hair was nasty, her teeth needed brushing, and her stomach was empty. All that mattered was her, him, and the fact they were together. His hand rubbing her leg, hers resting on top of his. Joined. But the ring of his phone cut through the sound of their laughter, causing them both to go silent once more.

With little more than a sigh, Levi hit the button on the wheel to pick up the call. "What's doing?"

"Meet-up planned and ready." The deep voice filled the cab. No intro, no greeting, but Levi must have known who it was.

"It's about time." His voice had a growl to it that

screamed frustration. Maybe she wasn't the only one tired of being on the road.

"This is one slippery human. It's taken us a bit to nail down the right place to set him up."

"Fine." Levi glanced her way before refocusing on the road. "Send me the coordinates."

"On it. Based on your last ping, we should be arriving at the same time or shortly after you."

"How shortly?"

"Half an hour, tops."

Levi's growl nearly shook the windshield. "And if this human gets there before you do?"

"Do what you need to do, kid. There's no retrieval on this one and no rules for elimination. The destroy order came down yesterday. Dude shows up, kill him."

"Understood." Levi hit the button to disconnect with a huff. Amy waited, silent and still, for him to say something. To explain what was happening. It wasn't until the phone pinged with the text that he even moved.

He set the navigation with one hand, keeping his eyes on the road. "Looks like another two hours, then we'll be able to stop."

Amy reached out and rubbed his leg the way he'd rubbed hers. "Thank the fates. You need to rest."

"What I need is to keep you safe."

"And if you don't sleep, you can't keep me safe."

He sighed. Probably frustrated again. "Amy—"

"Levi," she smarted back, exaggerating his name.

He growled and gave her a glare out of the corner of his eye that spoke of all the ways he'd probably like to punish her. She doubted abject arousal was his goal with that look, but it'd been a few days since she'd been touched by her mate. The deep, dark, demanding stare set her world on fire, not that she could do anything about it. Not for at least the two hours it took to get to this new place and enough time to wash off her funk.

Eventually, he sighed and seemed to slouch in his seat. "Fine. Once my brothers show up, I'll sleep."

Success. "That reminds me. We'll need to stop at a grocery store before we get to this safe house."

"What for?"

Amy nearly rolled her eyes. "Uh, food. You know, that stuff we eat to fuel our bodies."

"I've fed you." He sounded so defensive and petulant, she nearly laughed.

"Drive-through fast food isn't food."

Levi gaped at her for a moment before turning back to the road. "But it's got *food* in the title."

She growled, unable to help herself. The man was like a child. Arguing with her over something she knew way more about than he did. That growl shut him up good, though. She'd need to remember that.

"Fine," he spat after a long period of waiting, probably wishing she'd back down. Which she wouldn't…not about food. "We'll get groceries. But I choose the place and set the time. *No* screwing around in there."

"Fine. No screwing. Got it." She curled her lips into a smug smile when he glanced her way. "At least not in the grocery store."

A little over two hours later, they pulled up to a small parking lot in a small town just before the state line. What state, Amy wasn't even sure of anymore. They'd been driving all over the south for days with no discernable pattern. A trick to keep the bad guys from following them, Levi had said. A way to keep them confused. She assumed it worked, because she'd been in the car with him and still had no idea where they were.

Levi parked along the front of the building, blocking a fire lane. Not that she cared. Amy nearly threw open the door to escape the truck the second he put the thing in park, but he grabbed her arm and tugged her all the way across the seat to his side.

"Ten minutes. We grab what we need, and we get the hell out of here. Got it?"

He was so serious, so utterly in control. The fierceness in his voice and his expression had her shaking in her seat. "Yes, boss."

He growled and yanked her closer, kissing her deeply before letting her go. "I'm not your boss. I'm just trying to keep you with me. Alive."

Guilt was a heavy thing, but not too heavy for her to forget her empty belly. "Alive. Got it. I'll listen, I promise. Just let me get stuff to feed you. I'm trying to keep you with me and alive, too."

He ran a finger down the side of her face before sighing and looking out the windows. Soldier glare firmly in place. "Okay. Let's roll."

Once inside, she grabbed everything she could think she might need for a couple of good, hearty meals. Fresh vegetables, fruit, meat, starches, spices, and grains—she filled her cart easily, practically running through the aisles. Her shopping went without incident, though she had no idea if she met the ten-minute deadline or not. Levi didn't say anything, so she assumed she was under the wire on that one as they hurried toward the check stands.

He paid with cash, barely glancing at the cashier. Of course, she didn't seem to want to look at him either. There was a dangerous air about him, something dark and deadly even a human could probably sense. That girl would probably tell her friends stories of the customer who scared her just by existing.

"Ready?" Levi asked when they were through, his back stiff and his eyes already roaming the parking lot.

Amy nodded, feeling exposed behind the huge windows that lined the front of the store. Whether it was Levi's behavior or something else, she couldn't ignore the way her instincts were flaring hot and bright. Something was out there, hunting them. Tracking them down like prey. She could feel it. Sense it in a way. And she didn't like it.

Levi grabbed her hand and tugged her close, tucking her into the side of his body. He carried the bags and led them outside, walking faster than his normal pace. Amy did her best to keep up, but she stumbled a little over the rocky ground.

"Everything okay?" he asked, still not looking at her but at the horizon. Seeking out whatever danger was headed their way.

"I feel…vulnerable."

Levi unlocked the truck when they were still twenty feet away. Only the driver's side door. "Vulnerable how?"

Amy shrugged, suddenly wishing to be back in the truck and on the road again. "On display somehow."

Levi's voice was more growl than not as he rumbled, "Like you're being watched."

He directed her to his door, opening it wide for her. She hopped into the cab of the truck and scooted to the passenger side so he could follow her. "Yeah, I really do."

He checked that she was buckled in before setting the bags on the floorboard behind his seat and starting the engine.

"Me too. We need to get the hell out of here."

Seventeen

Levi pocketed his phone before walking into the kitchen. The guys were late, something that rarely happened. Something that made him want to toss his mate back in the truck and keep moving just in case, even if she'd probably kill him for it. And that was the last thing he wanted, considering his view.

Amy was cooking again, and Levi couldn't take his eyes off her. What was it about a woman—no, *this* woman—chopping and sautéing that was such a turn-on? A silly question when he really gave it a thought. When Amy worked in the kitchen, what she did was more than cooking. She was teasing the food, playing with it, making it do her bidding and become something more than just a mix of ingredients. It was a sensual act, a balance between taste and desire. The coming together of multiple senses in the most enticing way.

She was also dancing and humming as she cooked, shaking those hips of hers to the beat of the song playing over the speakers. Making that ass bounce in ways that should have been illegal…or at least against all properties of gravity or physics or some shit.

Fuck, he should have gone for the twelve orgasms before the food.

"Are you just going to sit there and stare?" She grinned over her shoulder, that look of happiness something he didn't ever want to disappear.

"Yes."

Her throaty chuckle made him grin as he settled in to enjoy his new favorite show. Her hair was still wet from her shower, the one she took while he patrolled and secured the property. He'd wanted to shower with her, but that would have led to sex, which would have led to distractions. He couldn't afford distractions. He felt relatively safe after walking the perimeter of the little mountain cabin he'd been sent to and investigating the woods behind the place, though his muscles were tense and his body at the ready.

Body and weapons.

He eyed the shotgun leaning against the wall by the kitchen entry. He preferred knives when fighting, but a human who didn't know what sort of creature Levi was would be more apt to fear him if he saw the gun. He'd checked it over, loaded it, and carried it with him through the house and around the property. Just in case. The fucker following them had gotten too close, and Levi wouldn't let that happen again.

Amy was in a deep grind—even dropping down a few inches to swing her ass in a way that made his cock sit up and take notice—when the sound of a car rolling over a gravel drive reached his ears.

Their gravel drive.

Levi was up and moving without a thought, without a word, his chair screeching as it flew backward. He grabbed the shotgun on his way out of the kitchen, pulling it to his shoulder as he stalked to the front door. He assumed the car coming was his brothers arriving as scheduled, but he couldn't be sure yet. He needed to be ready. No fucking way was anyone or anything getting to Amy tonight.

The car pulled to a stop outside, the engine sound dying out as someone turned off the ignition. Levi slipped into the shadows beside the door, listening. Amy had turned off the radio in the kitchen, but she hadn't followed him. They'd discussed what to do if something happened. She was to find a spot outside the action and stay put. Let him figure out the threat before she reacted. If there'd been a safe room in the place, he'd have made sure she was in it, but this cabin wasn't one of the president's emergency properties. Blasius Zenne had homes all around the world with safe rooms, food stockpiles, and weapons closets just in case a rival tried to come after him or one of his mates. A man in such a position of power was bound to have enemies. But they hadn't been close enough to one of those, apparently. This place was just a cabin in the woods…with a cellar full of guns and explosives. A Dire Wolf den, if Levi had to guess. Though, which of his brothers kept the place stocked, he didn't know.

Doors slammed, and the sound of multiple heavy footfalls on the gravel told Levi there was more than one person out there. Definitely not anyone trying to be sneaky, not that the noise changed Levi's plan. Gun pointed at the door, hackles raised, he stood in wait. Ready to take on any threat. Ready for battle.

But when the sound of heavy boots on wood hit the

porch, and the familiar scent of Dire Wolf met his nose, Levi sighed and dropped the gun.

"About time you got here," he said as he opened the door.

"Damn country roads made the trip a lot longer than planned." Mammon held up his fist for a bump before moving past.

"Didn't know I needed to teach you to drive, old man."

"You trying to egg me on, kid?"

Phego followed Mammon to the door but not through it. Not at first. The tall shifter paused and glanced around the cabin before walking inside, wary and looking for a fight. Typical, really. He didn't trust anyone, not even his own pack. Not that Levi could blame him. Phego's family had set him up to be murdered long before the Dires had formed a separate pack and come to this continent. That sort of thing would scar a man for life, no matter how long that life tended to be.

"What's that amazing smell?" Mammon asked, his eyes bright as he looked around.

"She's…making dinner." Levi fought back a streak of possessiveness. He didn't like another man commenting on his mate's food…didn't want him taking what Levi rightly saw as his. Not even a brother. Shit, he needed to get his wolf under control.

Mammon nudged Phego, grinning in a way that set Levi's teeth on edge. "Not the food, kid. The girl." He took a deep breath, a low rumble sounding as he exhaled. "She smells like a delight."

Levi's snarl was loud and sharp—a blatant warning to the two Dires. "Back off, man."

Mammon's easygoing smile dropped. He glared at what he had to see as a challenge, not backing down. "What the fuck's your problem?"

Phego cocked his head, his eyes swirling silver as his wolf pushed forward. "What'd you do…get your dick all up in there and risk our relations with her pack?"

Mammon hissed a curse, ignoring Levi's warning growl. "I thought we told you to control yourself for once."

The need to attack was a hard one to hold back, one Levi was definitely close to giving in to if the claws tearing through his fingertips were any indication. He didn't want to fight one of his brothers, but he had before, and he would again. For his mate.

But Amy walked into the room at that moment, looking a bit nervous but holding her head high. And glaring at Mammon as if the man had stolen her lunch.

"He's always very controlled around me."

Levi's lip turned up in what had to be a smirk. His little mate was coming to his defense. He didn't need it, had been dealing with these assholes for a millennia it seemed, but he liked it. There was an edge to her statement that appealed. He was definitely a possessive bastard; seeing Amy be possessive right back was hot as fuck.

He stared hard at Mammon, not releasing the shifter from his gaze even as he held out a hand for his mate. His *mate*. Not his toy, his dalliance, or his random hookup. She was his forever. He knew the reputation he'd earned over the years, but this wasn't some fling. This was the woman the fates had brought to him, the person who was his perfect match. He wasn't about to let his brothers think she was just some fling.

Amy crossed the room and grabbed his hand, letting him pull her into his side. Clinging to him and practically staking her claim. Mammon and Phego exchanged a look at that move, a fact that had Levi's smirk growing.

"Sorry, ma'am," Mammon said with a nod. "We didn't mean any disrespect."

"No apologies needed. At least not to me." She glanced up at Levi with a smile, looking so sweet and happy. But then her brow dropped, and her eyes hardened before she shot Mammon a glare that had him taking a step back. "But if you insult my mate again, there'll be no dinners for you. Ever. And I'm a really good cook."

Phego's eyes went wide as he shot a glance at Levi's neck. Bastard had to be able to see the reddened mating mark standing out against his skin loud and proud. Levi ran his fingers through Amy's long hair, tugging part of it over her shoulder. Making sure both men got a good look at his claiming bite on her skin as well, just to be sure they understood the mating was mutual, consensual, and permanent. He wouldn't put it past them to claim Levi had coerced the woman somehow.

"Why didn't you tell us?" Phego asked, glancing from Levi to Amy and back again.

Levi shook his head. "You really need to ask that?"

Phego sighed and glanced at Mammon, the two of them having a mind meld sort of conversation without words. "Thaus is going to love this."

Levi didn't miss the sarcastic tone to his voice. "Thaus can get his panties out of that twist any time now."

"Who's Thaus?" Amy asked.

Shit, she was going to have to meet Thaus one day, would need to meet all his brothers. Including Luc. What felt like a shard of ice skittered along his spine. In terms of potential disasters, it would be way worse for her to meet Luc. Levi was certain Bez hadn't grown the balls to introduce his mate to the shifter they all saw as Alpha, and Sariel had been mated to the Dire for more than a year.

"Thaus is one of my brothers. Part of my pack." Levi ignored the raised eyebrow Phego shot him. "He's a little… tougher than the rest of us."

She looked over each man in turn, her face solid and stoic. Not giving anything away. Levi wished he could see the three of them as she saw them, though her mumbled *let's hope not* gave him a little insight into how she sized up the men around her. And a peek at her bravery once more.

After a tense moment Levi hoped never to have to repeat in his lifetime, Amy took a deep breath and pasted a smile on her face. "C'mon, boys. So long as no one's pounding down the door to kill me, I might as well feed you."

Levi snatched her, almost clinging to her and snarling viciously. Amy froze in his arms as the other two men in the room growled long and loud, matching Levi in tone. She didn't say anything, but Levi could feel the tension in her shoulders, the way her hands shook as she grasped his wrists. They were scaring her.

That knowledge allowed Levi to be the first to shake off the aggression and regain control of his animal side. He set her back on the floor and took a step away, feeling a bit sheepish.

"Sorry," he said. "But the idea of someone coming to kill you is…"

He trailed off, his heart breaking at the thought. His rage billowing through him like smoke. It was Phego who voiced at least part of what he wanted to say.

"It's abhorrent."

"Yeah," Mammon agreed. "What he said. And it's not happening on our watch."

Amy's round eyes met Levi's, her surprise evident. "Well, I appreciate that."

Levi sighed, still trying to stop his heart from racing.

"We're a little protective of our own. And you, being an Omega, qualify."

Phego shot him another weird look, one Levi ignored again. He knew the shifter would have questions and concerns, but he wasn't ready to deal with all that yet. He had a mate to protect.

"Yeah, Omegas are family," Mammon said with a grin. "But your unfortunate mating to this asshole cemented it. You're ours, baby. Get used to it."

Levi snorted a laugh as Amy sighed.

"More men. That's just what I need in my life. More men."

"Hey." Phego shrugged. "We've got one female in our ranks. I mean, Bez and Sariel rarely leave his compound in Texas so we don't see much of her unless we head down by them, but she counts."

"Lovely." Amy headed for the kitchen, her head high once more and that ass swinging. "So it's me and this woman to help balance out the testosterone of your pack. I bet we'll have lots to talk about when I meet her."

Phego and Mammon blocked Levi as soon as Amy left the room.

"You didn't tell her?" Phego asked, glaring hard.

Levi shrugged, avoiding his glare. "Didn't have time."

Mammon scoffed at that cheap answer, as he should have. "Gee, how much time does it take to say, *Oh, by the way, I'm a Dire Wolf. We're supposed to be extinct so don't tell anyone, and I live like a motherfucking gypsy traveling from place to place because I can't stand to be stuck in one spot for long?*"

Levi wanted to argue with him, but he couldn't. He should have told her already. Should have explained everything to her. But he could already see the pitfalls of their lives coming together. She'd fought him to stay in that tiny town, had refused to go willingly at first because of her business and her family. Meanwhile, Levi had never voluntarily stayed in the same place for more than a month, had never even considered actually owning anything more than what he could throw in his truck and haul around with him. At least, not until he met Amy.

"You are a jackass," Phego barked, pulling Levi from his thoughts. "You had three motherfucking days in your truck. Seems like plenty of time and opportunity to me."

Levi growled and moved as if to confront the bastard, but quick footsteps and the smell of his mate approaching had him dropping back.

"Boys." Amy's sharp reprimand had all three men spinning her way. "Quit arguing and come eat. Levi's been forcing me to survive on nasty hamburgers and soggy fries for the past three days."

"Sounds familiar." Mammon followed her toward the kitchen, pausing just long enough to grab Levi's forearm in a show of respect. Eyes on Levi's, the shifter nodded once as they gripped one another. That expression, that nod, sent a shot of relief through Levi. His brothers would accept Amy, would accept their mating. Not that he'd worried they wouldn't, but… Okay, he'd worried they wouldn't. He wanted his pack and his mate. Hell, he wanted her pack, too. For the first time in his long life, Levi wanted a large group around him and his mate. A protective circle, if you would. Though no one would protect his mate better than him.

Phego followed Mammon, gripping Levi's arms and nodding once. Respectful but also a little…dangerous. Already, he was willing to throw down for his new sister, that much was obvious by the glare in his eyes. And Levi appreciated it. His brothers were there to help, and they would guard an Omega with their lives. But an Omega mated to one of their own? There were no limits to what they would do to keep her safe. No boundaries.

They would eliminate the threat.

Levi nearly shook with restrained laughter when he walked into the kitchen behind the two Dires, though. Both men stood awkwardly by the table, watching almost helplessly as Amy moved about. Waiting for something she had no idea she needed to give them.

Direction.

Finally, Amy noticed them standing together and gave them a strange glance. "You can sit, you know."

Mammon's eyes shot to Levi for a moment. "No, ma'am, we can't. But we'd be happy to help you with whatever you need."

Amy stared, her mouth opening and closing when she couldn't find the words. The pan she'd been holding drooping as her grip slackened. Finally, to keep her from hurting herself and ruining whatever it was that smelled so damn good, Levi put her out of her misery. He strode across the room and grabbed the pan, setting it back on the stove and nudging her toward the table.

"Sit, Amy. You cooked. Let us at least serve you."

She shook her head, the movements jerky and off as if she couldn't quite understand the words. But then she smiled. "Well, that's a first."

"Did Leviathan forget the manners we taught him?" Phego growled and pointed a warning finger. Protective already. "She's your mate, son. Not your maid."

Levi put his hands up before moving to pull said mate to his chest. Using her to shield himself, but also taking advantage of her closeness to press his hips against that ass. He couldn't resist it. "I didn't forget the rules, man. She made me one meal, and I cleaned up after we ate. Otherwise, we've been on the road the whole time. It's hard to show manners when your food comes through the window of your truck."

Phego glanced from Levi to Amy and back again before giving them a nod. "Fine. But don't let us hear about you slacking."

"Never." Levi kissed the top of Amy's head and directed her to the table, pulling out her chair. "Sit, please."

And she did, still looking sort of shell-shocked. Growing up with twelve brothers must have really set her mind about how men would treat her. Good thing for her, she mated into the Dires.

Levi served the food family style before settling in at the table next to his mate. He even scooched his chair over to be closer to her, needing the comfort of her presence to relax. His brothers were here, and they'd do everything they could to help him keep her safe. He knew this, but he still worried. Somehow, the human tracking Amy and her family had gotten past the pack, his mate, and his brothers. Not as successfully as certain subsets of soldiers probably could, but enough to be seen as a real threat. That wasn't normal.

Still, his brothers would help. Already, they were falling under Amy's charms. He'd never heard so many pleases and thank yous in his life, especially not from Mammon. But the shifter seemed smitten with his curvy mate. He praised her food and laughed at her jokes, used his napkin and even kept his elbows off the table. The charmer.

"Can I get you boys anything else?" Amy asked as she rose from the table. The three men stood in response, earning a raised eyebrow from the female.

"No, thank you, ma'am," Mammon answered.

Levi rolled his eyes at Mammon's sucking up. "We'll take care of cleanup. Why don't you go get ready for bed? I know you're tired."

She hummed and nodded, looking sleepy but happy. "You're joining me, right?"

"Of course." Levi gave her a quick hug and a kiss to the top of the head. "Just give me a few minutes to talk business first."

She headed down the hall with a small wave to the other two men. Levi made sure to smile until she was gone, waiting for her to close the bedroom door behind her before dropping the expression.

Time to get to work.

"What's doing?"

The three sat back at the table, food forgotten. There was a different vibe in the air, a specific tension that came from the shifters when their attention switched to business matters. It was as if the energy of the cabin knew they'd gone into military mode and were solely focused on strategy and planning.

"It's time to bait the fucker," Mammon said, keeping his voice low. "He's a sneaky SOB and keeps slipping past us. We need to draw him out."

Levi definitely didn't like the thought of that. "Bait him with what?"

Phego cocked his head, probably at the growl in his brother's voice, but he stayed silent. Waiting. Mammon at least had the decency to look at the floor. A fact that made Levi's stomach drop. There was only one reason his brothers would be acting that way. The logical choice of what—or rather whom—to use as bait was an obvious one, years of strategic training and war methodology telling him exactly what need to be done. But strategy was now colored by the fact that the logical bait in question was his mate. The only one he'd ever have.

Strategy and logic be damned. "No fucking way."

Mammon sighed. "Kid, there is no—"

"I'm not your fucking kid, and I said no." Levi jumped to his feet and stormed toward the hall, ready to leave this shit behind him. "Call me when you come up with a better plan."

"He'll hunt her forever." Phego's words drew Levi up short. "He'll hunt her every second of every day until he gets her or we get him. This guy isn't some normal stalker, and I don't think he's alone. We believe he knows she's a shifter, and he's been prepping her for his plans. Training her to think of him as kind so he can manipulate her into doing what he wants. We fucked up his plans when we took her away from him, and now he's out for vengeance and to take back what he sees as his."

"She's not his," Levi said, the snarl behind his words filling the kitchen with a warning his brothers didn't need nor deserve.

"You know that, she knows that, and we know that. But this guy?" Phego paused, his silence making Levi turn. His face serious as he stared at his brother. "He doesn't give a fuck."

Levi clenched his fists, ready to punch something. "He's a fucking human. A kindergarten teacher. How dangerous can he be?"

Phego didn't even have to look at his phone to begin ticking items off. "He's not military, but he's trained in survival and tracking. He hasn't hired mercenaries, but he's somehow been able to convince other humans to join him. He's charismatic, or Amy wouldn't have been so upset by his deception. And he is completely, utterly obsessed with her if the scent trails he left are any indication, which I think they are."

Mammon grunted his agreement. "He won't ever give up, and he's building small armies around him to make it harder to determine the true threat. You've got two choices, Levi. Bait him to draw him out and kill him quickly. Or keep running."

Levi sighed, gritting his teeth. Knowing Phego was right, but hating to admit it. Still, he wasn't stupid.

"Call in Thaus. If we do this, I want him beside me." He swallowed hard, squeezing his eyes shut to block out the truth of what they were about to do. "I want him beside Amy."

And then he headed for the bedroom. For his mate.

Eighteen

Two showers in one day wasn't Amy's norm, but after two days without, she felt the need to catch up. When she was finished in the ensuite bathroom, she hung up her towel and headed to the bedroom. She wanted to find one of Levi's shirts to sleep in, something soft and comfortable that would smell like him. The need to join with him, to reconnect physically, burned through her. Her body practically itched for more of her mate, but with his brothers in the same house, she wasn't sure if she'd get him anytime soon.

But Levi was already in the bedroom when she emerged from the steam-filled bathroom. She froze in midstep, unable to move, barely able to breathe. Just the sight of him made her heart race, made her arousal spike. Damn, she wanted him. Needed him, really. The mating imperative was controlling her in a way nothing ever had.

Amy assumed he'd say something about the fact that she wore nothing but a towel, or that he'd do something about it. She could almost picture him stripping the towel from her still-damp body and tossing her on the bed. Could practically feel his lips on her breast as he chased a water droplet or two.

But instead, Levi stood by the door, growling softly. Staring, sure, but not really *at* her. She wasn't even sure he saw her. He scowled at some unknown thought, his eyes angry as he glared past her. This man was not her Levi, not the one who whispered sweet things to her and joked about his prowess in bed. No, this was soldier Levi, the man she'd first met in her kitchen, the one who'd thrown her over his shoulder to steal her away. The one who'd scared her.

Something was very, very wrong.

"Levi?" Amy kept her voice soft as she took a single step forward, but Levi's snarl shoved her back.

"Not yet." Clipped. Harsh. Demanding. Definitely not the man she'd come to know outside of the soldier. So she waited, cold and dripping in her towel but patient. Her mate needed a moment, and she'd give that to him. Give him a thousand moments if it meant tucking the soldier away and getting the man she was falling for back. Even if every second caused her worry to double, then triple.

It took far longer than Amy would have liked, but eventually, his shoulders lost their stiffness and his eyes softened. And yet, she waited, watching for more. The biggest sign that he'd tucked the soldier away for the time being came when he stopped growling. And still, she waited. He'd made no move toward her, given her no sign that she was welcomed or wanted. She'd give him more time, knowing he still needed it. He'd let her know when he was ready for her; that, she could be sure of. She refused to push him.

When he finally took a deep breath and spoke, the words were soft. His voice almost defeated, belying the strength behind his statement. "I'd never let anything happen to you."

"I know," she replied, anxiety slipping around her throat. His eyes locked on hers, still angry, still hard, but something else burned there. Something more along the lines of fear.

Levi pushed off the wall, stalking closer, not releasing her from his stare. "This guy, he's slippery."

That sounded ominous. "Okay."

"He's been able to hide from you, your pack, my brothers. He's snuck up on us once…he's not going to be easy to flush out."

He looked so fierce and yet so scared. An odd combination for sure, and one that didn't quite fit. But then the pieces began to fall together, a picture emerging in her mind of what had made her mate so pissed off and worried that he could barely speak.

A picture that honestly scared Amy more than she cared to admit. "You want to use me as bait."

"Fuck no, I don't." He grabbed her by the hips, his hands rough, his grip needy. Pulling her against him. Clinging to her in a way that reeked of desperation. "Jesus, doll. That's the very last thing I want. But my brothers think it's the best course of action, and it's probably the only way we'll get this guy on our terms. Otherwise…"

Amy closed her eyes, waiting for what she knew was coming. Surrendering to the need to hear the words when Levi couldn't find his voice. "Otherwise, he'll never stop, and we'll have to keep running from him until he finally screws up."

Levi's whimper gutted her, had her gripping him harder, wishing there was another way. But she knew why, she understood the reasoning—they couldn't make a life together with this guy chasing them.

Amy pulled on every thread of bravery she'd earned

throughout her life, every bit of strength that came from being the daughter of an Alpha, the Omega of a pack, and the sister of twelve older brothers. She gathered the determination she'd cultivated as she'd pushed to leave her pack, the faith in herself she'd fed by starting her own business, and the strength she'd earned refusing to give in when things had scared her.

And then she shrugged. "So I have to be bait."

Amy died a little when Levi looked away, hiding his eyes from her, though not quite soon enough. That flash of pain on his face, that fury and helplessness—it killed her. Made her ache with a need to soothe him. She ran a hand down his cheek until he finally met her gaze again, until the green color she'd grown so attached to focused back on her.

"I trust you," she whispered, infusing every syllable with her faith. But sometimes faith wasn't enough.

"Maybe you shouldn't."

"Maybe you should trust yourself a little more." She wrapped both arms around his neck, pulling him down to press her forehead to his. Needing him close. "Would you hurt me, Levi?"

"Never." A whisper of sound, a promise that screamed.

"Would you let anyone else hurt me?"

His growl was fierce. "No fucking way."

The tone—the claim in his voice—made bits of her come alive. Important bits. The ones that hadn't been taken care of in days. She'd been told sex was a stress reliever, a way of letting go of your problems and giving in to nothing but instinct and sensation. She was about to find out firsthand.

She pulled out of his arms, turning her back to him. Looking at him over her shoulder as she crept toward the bed. "Do you trust me, Levi?"

"Of course."

"Then trust yourself. You'd never do anything I didn't want you to or that would put me in danger." With a simple flick of her wrist, she pulled the towel from her body and dropped it to the floor. Completely naked, the only sensation on her flesh the feel of his eyes watching her, she crawled across the bed. Kept each move slow and sensual, rolling smoothly like the glide of honey on skin.

Levi stepped closer, his thighs forcing her calves to spread to accommodate him, his hand coming to rest on her lower back. "I hate that you'd be in danger."

"You'll be with me, right?" She stared down at the comforter, holding herself perfectly still for him. Wanting more than his simple touch but knowing he needed a minute. Knowing she did, too. They had things to say. Promises to make.

"Every second." He ran a hand up the length of her spine, pressing her shoulders down. She followed that subtle direction, turning her head to place her cheek against the mattress. Putting her ass in the air. Opening herself for his observation.

"Fuck, you're so beautiful." One hand still flat between her shoulders, he slid the other down the length of her back and over her ass, stopping to grab and smack lightly. Amy kept her head pressed against the mattress, letting him see. Letting him touch as she shivered and clutched at the bedding. Wanting him in a way that was almost painful.

But Levi never disappointed her. He slipped his fingers inside of her, plunging in and out slowly. Teasingly, almost. The wet sounds of her body taking part of his making her shake with desire, making him growl. The hand on her shoulders disappeared only to find a home on her thigh, wrapping around with a grip just shy of painful. He pulled, yanking her to the edge of the bed, putting her right where he wanted her. Never breaking the rhythm of the fingers inside her.

"I won't let anyone else touch you," he whispered, his growl adding depth to his words and making her clench with need. "I *will* keep you safe."

"Why?" she asked, pleaded, really. She knew the reason, but she needed to hear it. Felt as if he needed to say it, too.

He ruthlessly pressed on her clit with his knuckle as he added another finger inside. She trembled, unable to hold still but trying so hard not to pull away. Not to hump his hand, either, though she wanted to. Wanted to do whatever it took to get off at that moment. He had her keyed up, completely on edge. And she wanted to fall.

His hand disappeared from her thigh, and the sound of him unfastening his jeans broke the heavy silence between them. A sound that made Amy sigh and sag. Soon, just a few more seconds. But those seconds ran long, the time it took for Levi to free himself seeming near endless. Levi grunted as if irritated, as if he couldn't wait a moment longer. And maybe he couldn't, because with his jeans still hugging his thighs, he yanked his fingers from between her legs and flipped her on her back. Crawled over her and pinned her down. Their hands joined by her head, his heavy dick lined up and ready.

"Why will I keep you safe? Because you're mine." He ground against her, sliding just the tip inside before pulling away. "Only mine."

Which was exactly what she needed to hear. "Yours."

Amy gasped as he thrust inside with a groan, trying to pull her hands away so she could grab and touch and claw. But Levi wouldn't release her, wouldn't give her an inch to move from where he wanted her. Amy lay completely at his mercy, and she loved it.

He was so deep, so thick and hard inside of her. Every withdrawal had her begging him for more, every push in causing her to cry or growl. Nothing mattered but the feel of him on her, in her, the acceptance of his body ruling hers. She couldn't feel anything but him. Couldn't hear or see anything but his sounds, his face. His every breath owned her, his every move making her want more. In that moment, he was her world, and she was his. Their connection solid, exclusionary, and deep. Exactly what she'd wanted.

The sex was quick and rough. A reclaiming of sorts. The feel of Levi's clothes against her skin, knowing he was too impatient to strip them off, was more than enough to push her to the point of no return in record time. The deep thrusts he gave her, the way he stroked in and out with purpose, made her rise that much faster. Amy came first, clinging to Levi's shirt and sighing his name as her body clenched around him. He lost his rhythm when she arched into him, jackhammering her into the mattress. Knocking the headboard into the wall until he came with a groan. Until he cursed and hissed and shook with the pleasure of his surrender.

Levi collapsed on top of her, the two cuddled in a sort of obscene, sweaty puppy pile. Exactly as they both desired.

Amy ran her fingers through his hair for several minutes before whispering, "Better now?"

He sighed, rolling slightly to take his weight off her, moving down the mattress enough to rest his forehead against her chest. To nuzzle her breasts. To lick a trail along the top of them.

"I hate that you'll be in danger." He wrapped his lips around a nipple, drawing it into his mouth after two swipes of his tongue.

She arched into his touch, groaning softly as tingles shot

through to her spine. "I won't be. You'll be watching out for me."

He sighed and pressed his hips into hers, already growing hard again. "I know, but it's not how I would have wanted this to play out."

Amy wrapped her legs around his waist, pulling him up the length of her, peppering his face and lips with soft kisses before smiling. "I'll make sure to grab my skillet. It seemed to work on you."

He growled and rolled with her, ending with her on top. "How very *Tangled* of you."

That made her pause. "You've seen *Tangled*?"

He shrugged, not looking the least bit embarrassed. "I like Disney movies. The animation is kickass."

"Why doesn't that surprise me?" She pushed up to a sitting position and settled on his hips, straddling him, rocking slowly as she took him inside her again. On her terms this time. Damn, he felt so good like this. Slid so much deeper, it seemed. Levi thrust up, lifting her, knocking her off-balance. Amy fell back, putting her hands on his thighs to brace herself, groaning as the new position forced her to feel all sorts of new sensations.

Levi chuckled all low and husky. "Oh, now this could be fun."

Amy glanced down the length of her body to where they were joined, watching as his erection disappeared inside her. Fuck, that was hot. The position left her breasts and hips open for Levi, giving him room to play with the parts of her that begged for his attention. Room he took full advantage of. He pressed his thumb against her clit, rubbing harder with every stroke until he made her shudder. Made her clench and moan. Made her bounce up and down on his dick as she chased the release that was already so close.

"Rapunzel, Rapunzel. You've let down your hair." Levi pulled on the ends of her hair, softly at first. The pressure growing firmer as she rode him. And fuck, that little bit of control, that tiny bit of demand, was even hotter than watching him slide inside her.

She groaned and sat deeper, riding his hand and his dick. Already so close to coming, she could barely keep up a rhythm without his help. "I'll play the part of Rapunzel if you'll be my Flynn Ryder."

Levi grinned and grabbed her thighs as if she might need the extra support. And knowing him, she did.

"I didn't want to have to do this, but you leave me no choice." His thrusts grew stronger, deeper, his movements making her curl over and moan as pleasure shot straight through her. As the depth and the speed and the constant assault against her clit finally pushed her over the edge and let her crash around him. "Here comes the smolder."

And boy, could that man smolder.

Nineteen

The morning came too soon for Levi. For the Dires as well, it seemed. Breakfast was a quiet, almost somber affair. Even though he tried to stop Amy by offering to do it himself, she cooked for them again. Working at the stove seemed to keep her calm, so Levi didn't push the matter. Still, he kept his eyes on her as he sat with Phego and Mammon, doing his best not to grab his mate and run.

Even Mammon and Phego were more reserved than usual. Mammon stared hard at the table, glancing at Amy every now and again with a frown. Phego slouched in his seat, watching Levi more than Amy. Doubting him, it seemed. But Levi had to stay neutral, had to follow orders and do what was the right choice strategically…no matter how much he hated the plan. He wanted this guy off their tail so he and Amy could go off and…do something. Live happily ever after? Have a couple of pups? Shit, he hadn't thought about any of that. When Bez found his mate in Sariel, he moved her to his Texas compound. Gave her stability, took her from a pack that didn't appreciate her to his home. Levi had no compound. He had no home of his own. He had a sense of wanderlust that had dogged him since the first time he'd looked out at the horizon—and a mate with roots as deep as any he'd ever known.

He was utterly, totally screwed.

Which was really not what he needed to be thinking about at that moment. Thaus was on his way, and Levi knew that once he arrived, the Dires would finalize the bait-and-switch plan and put it into motion. Would set up Amy as bait for this bastard to hunt.

Strategy had never been so fucking stupid.

"Thank you, Miss Amy." Phego smiled up at Levi's mate as she set a plate of eggs and bacon before him. The expression on his face, the respect there, left a humbling impression on Levi. His brothers treated Amy like family from the moment they'd mated, and that was something he wouldn't forget. Not even when they offered her up to the bastard chasing them.

There really should have been whiskey in his coffee.

"Yes," Mammon said as he nodded toward the plate she offered him. "Thank you so much."

"You're welcome." Amy came to sit on Levi's lap, snuggling into his chest. He held her close, breathing her in. Wishing for time to speed up or stop, for this to be over with.

"What time should Thaus get here?" Levi asked, grabbing Amy's hip and pulling her in even tighter. Not willing to have an inch of space between them.

Mammon glanced at the clock. "Anytime now, I'd guess."

Amy kissed his neck, her fingers scratching through the hair on the back of his head. An oddly calming sensation that did little to make Levi relax.

With a sigh, she stopped scratching and sagged away from him. "I'm going to get cleaned up."

"Okay." Levi held on to her, though, kissing her lips one last time before he allowed her to leave his lap. He couldn't help himself; he wanted her with him every second until this was over. Wanted her hidden away in his nonexistent compound, safe from the dangers lurking outside.

Wanted her to know every secret he had.

With the history of his breed weighing heavy on his mind and the knowledge that his mate was in the dark about it all tugging at his heart, he sighed and twined his fingers with hers to keep her still. "But I want to talk to you before we make a move on this plan."

Amy smiled and kissed his nose, oblivious to the tornado brewing inside of him, then dragged herself to her feet. She even ran her fingers along his shoulders as she headed for the door as if she couldn't stand to be parted from him. Levi understood that feeling. His wolf especially didn't like watching her walk away, didn't want to be too far from her, but he couldn't crowd her. They were all on edge, and she needed her privacy as much as anyone. Privacy that would last exactly ninety seconds before he checked on her.

As soon as Amy left the room, Mammon sighed and frowned. "You need to tell her about us."

Levi sighed. "I know. I'm going to."

"Maybe she's never heard the old legends." Phego shrugged, sitting back in his chair. "A lot of packs ignore those tales."

"One can only hope." Levi looked to the ceiling, trying to get his words straight in his head. Dire Wolves, millennia on earth, the never-ending moving, the constant fighting. Amy wasn't going to be happy about some of that. She was a stable wolf, one who loved her pack even though she needed her own room to grow. His lifestyle was at complete odds with that.

Mammon tapped the side of his fist on the table, watching Levi with dark eyes. A sign Levi wasn't going to like what came out of his mouth.

"I know this bait thing is—"

"Don't." Levi's word came out on a snarl, making Mammon's eyes go wide. "You know nothing."

But Mammon was never one to take a hint. "Just because I don't have a mate doesn't mean I don't—"

"I can feel her emotions." That shut him up. "We exchanged mating bites, so I can sense her. I know where she is, and I feel a shadow of what she does. Do you have any idea what it's like to know your partner is terrified but putting on a brave face? To be absolutely sure of it? Especially when what they're terrified of is something you're going to help lead?"

Mammon just shook his head, unable to hold Levi's stare. "No, I don't."

"Exactly." The sound of a car rolling across gravel interrupted the face-off. *Perfect fucking timing, Thaus.* Levi sighed and grabbed his cup of coffee. "About time he got here."

A car door slammed, and the sound of footsteps on gravel floated through the kitchen. Quiet and moody, the Dires kept their seats, all probably a little too stressed over this situation. Plus, as far as their manners went, greeting a brother was unnecessary. Thaus wouldn't even pause at the closed front door.

But it was when the sound of shoes on the wood porch steps hit Levi's ears that his wolf exploded to the forefront of his mind and all hell broke loose.

Shoes…soft-soled, like the kind you ran or exercised in. Not the lug-soled boots all Dire Wolves tended to wear.

"Amy." Levi gasped the word on a whisper—an automatic sort of sound made by breath and fear and rage coming together inside him. It escaped without thought, without effort. And then the snarling began.

Levi was up and running for the front of the house in a heartbeat, the table flipped and chairs broken as his brothers followed. Amy stood in the hallway, right in front of the door as if she was going to answer it. Moving closer even as she spun to see what all the commotion was about. Levi's heart skipped a beat as his world slowed. He wouldn't reach her in time; he couldn't. And he knew it.

The glass on the door exploded inward with the blast of what sounded like a shotgun. Pieces of wood, glass, and metal all flew into the room, hitting Amy. Stopping Levi's heart as the scent of her blood infiltrated his senses. She fell backward with a scream, eyes closed and arms up as if to protect herself. To ward off more of the debris.

Levi dropped to his knees and slid across the wood floor, ending almost directly under Amy and catching her before she made it to the hard floor. Cradling her body in his arms. Phego and Mammon shifted on the fly and raced past them, bursting through the door, their heavy wolves knocking it off the hinges.

Motherfucker. The bastard had gotten the jump on them. Again.

More gunshots joined the cacophony of the morning, and two additional car doors slammed. The fake kindergarten teacher had arrived and brought friends, it seemed.

Levi needed to get out there, was desperate to put teeth and claws into action against this fucker, but Amy needed him. She was hurt. His mate's blood was the only thing he could see, the only scent on the air. It enraged him and his wolf. Made them both ready to hunt. To kill. To seek vengeance.

Amy grabbed his arm, breathing heavy. Levi hated seeing her hurt, but there wasn't much he could do except drag her toward the back of the house. Another handful of shots fired, the round ending with the surprised whimper of one of his brothers. Levi roared toward the open door, his hands curving into paws, fingertips lost to claws. This fucker was going to pay…as soon as he made sure Amy was safe.

"Go," Amy said, pushing on his shoulder. She winced and grabbed her arm, blood seeping between her fingers. "It's nothing. They need you."

Levi glanced toward the door again, then dragged her a few more inches toward the kitchen. "You need me."

"I need you to kill that guy so we can stop this nonsense."

The fierceness in her eyes, the surety, was the only thing that could have convinced him she was telling the truth. Amy was right—he needed to get out there and fight so they could end this.

Levi lifted her into his arms and carried her up the first three steps of the staircase. He set her on the landing, tucking her into the corner. Blocking her in on two-and-a-half sides. It wasn't perfect, but it would have to do for now. He didn't want her too far away, and he doubted she'd want that either.

When Levi was sure she was as comfortable as he could make her, he rushed to the side table and yanked open the drawer. He passed over the SOG SEAL knife just like his own, knowing it wasn't enough. But a small pistol sat inside, one he'd made sure was loaded and ready. Just in case.

It was *just in case* time.

"Here." He made sure the safety was off before handing it to his wary mate. "Stay right here by the stairs. If you need us, scream. We'll come no matter what. But shoot first."

"It's okay. I'll scream or shoot. Go."

Levi kissed the top of her head. "Shoot *first*, scream second, ask questions later. Even if you hit one of us, we'll heal. Okay?"

"Levi," she cried, her hands shaking and her eyes filling with tears.

"None of that." He wiped her face and pressed the gun into her hands more firmly. "Not a single one of us would blame you if you hit us. Promise me—shoot first."

She nodded, looking so small and scared at that moment, it ripped at something in his chest. Levi bent over and kissed her forehead, closing his eyes to stop them from burning.

"Be safe, doll."

He didn't wait for a response, running outside before he lost his will. Leaving his heart behind.

Time to get to work.

Three men stood on the driveway, tucked behind the car they'd rolled up in. Humans, by the look of them. One, the man they'd identified as Randall or Gavin, shot toward the house as Levi raced across the porch. Guns didn't usually worry shifters because they could heal faster than they bled out most of the time, but these guys were different. He could sense it, knew it from the way they'd tracked and found Amy and him. Levi would not be underestimating them.

Phego sat still in wolf form, tucked into the far corner of the porch. Mammon lay curled against a porch support beam in his human form, clutching his arm. Blood splatter painted the porch with bright red polka dots, and a puddle was growing underneath Mammon. More than the shifter would have expected. Way more.

Levi ducked and hurried to his side, thankful the damn roof supports were as thick as they were but knowing he'd be hit if he wasn't careful.

"What's doing?"

Mammon growled as another round of gunfire sounded and broke a couple of spindles a little too close for comfort. "Fuckers have something on or in the bullets. This shit ain't healing right."

"Fuck." Levi ducked as a bullet made the handrail right above his head shatter. "We need to disarm them."

Phego shifted human, crouching behind the corner post. "No shit. How you planning on doing that if those bullet wounds don't heal?"

And wasn't that the question of the morning? "I don't know, but we'd better do something and quick."

Before Phego could answer, the gunshots stopped and that lying bastard of a so-called kindergarten teacher spoke up.

"Give us the bitch, and we might just let you freaks of nature live."

Levi practically roared, his growl making the very structure of the porch shake.

"Well, well, well… Someone knows our secret. Or at least part of it." Phego's eyes swirled silver, the Dire in him making himself known. "Time to put together a new plan, because we sure as fuck aren't doing what they want now."

"Shit." Amy dropped the gun and clutched her arm. The blood ran over her fingers, pooling on the floor below.

She took a deep breath, trying to think of what she could do that wouldn't risk her mate. She didn't know a lot of first aid, not much more than the stuff they showed on television. As a shifter, she healed fast. Way fast. Far faster than the damaged flesh of her arm was currently healing. She'd never felt so much pain or seen so much of her own blood, neither of which helped the panic she was fighting. The sight of her mate racing around the corner and into the hallway had made every instinct flare to life inside of her, had made adrenaline surge through her veins. He'd looked ready to kill as he'd raced toward her…and then the world had exploded.

The sound of her blood dripping onto the wood floor was enough to make her decision for her. She needed to get up and seek help. Levi had said to scream, but she didn't want to distract him or his brothers. If she could move close enough to the door, she could probably just say his name and he'd come running. But first, she needed a towel or something to wrap around her bloodied arm. Pressure… On television, they always talked about needing to keep pressure on the wound.

When Amy got to her feet, though, the room decided to dance for her. She gripped the newel-post for balance, nearly falling down the three steps to the main level. She stood stock-still and waited it out, hoping she didn't throw up all over her own feet. The sick feeling, the balance issues… What the hell was wrong with her?

When the room stopped spinning, she gritted her teeth and tried to walk toward something stable. It took only four steps before her head grew too heavy to hold up. The room spun again as she fell into the wall, and her joints began to ache in a way she'd never experienced. Shit, she needed Levi, but she couldn't remember what he'd told her to do. He was outside, fighting for her, but was he in the front or the back? Where was Phego and…that other one? The one with the nice manners and bad attitude? And why couldn't she remember his name?

Her stomach lurched again, and her hands began to shake. Maybe if she just went out the front door. It was close and already open just a bit. Which was good, because she was pretty sure she wouldn't be able to figure out how to use the handle thing. Not without help, at least. She tried to scoot, keeping her butt on the wood floor, but every move made her vision blur and her focus fade. Crawling might be better. Crawling was basically lying down and sliding on a floor like this. Yes, crawling was good. Being close to the ground was a fine plan.

She almost celebrated the first bit she gained. Almost cried over the second, but she kept moving. Kept crawling… sort of.

But as she slithered down the wall to gain another few inches, something dropped right where she needed to go. Blocked and without enough strength to turn another way. She was about to attempt a maneuver around the tan thing in her way when rough hands grabbed her shoulders and lifted her to a sitting position. She gagged and moaned, her head swiveling as she tried to get a good look at who was holding her. It wasn't Levi, but he was…familiar. She knew his scent, and she was okay with him being there. She was safe.

"Shhh," the man hissed softly as he wrapped her undamaged arm around his neck and helped her to her feet. "Let's get you out of here so we can take care of that arm."

She wanted to nod, but her head felt too heavy. Instead, she rested it against his chest and let him lead her toward the kitchen. He smelled of shifter and something else. Something like coffee. Something that reminded her of food. Breakfast, maybe. A restaurant or diner…

Her diner. Of course.

"What are you doing here?" she asked, her words muddy and thick even to her own ears. Zeke—the shifter who'd been sitting at her counter for the week before Levi came crashing into her life, the drifter who'd hit on her, chatted with her, and eaten her food—walked her into the kitchen…heading toward the back door.

"I'm here to help you, Armaita."

Amy's head cleared enough to revolt at the use of that word. Armaita…pack name…not pack. Zeke was not pack and not mate. She expected her wolf to growl at that thought, but she was met with an odd, uncomfortable silence.

Amy tried to pull away from the shifter, but Zeke had a solid hold on her and she didn't have the strength or coordination left to put up much of a struggle. She didn't even know if she'd be able to stand on her own, but something inside of her, something deep and instinctual, screamed at her to try. To keep fighting. To refuse to give up.

"I don't think you're supposed to be here," she said, not quite sure why that rectangle of light leading outside worried her so.

"Oh, on that you're wrong." Zeke dragged her into the cold, cruel sunlight of a winter's day. She had one brief moment of clarity, of instinct and fear and Levi's words coming together to warn her about what was probably happening, before Zeke lifted her onto his shoulders and began running across the snow-covered backyard. Taking her away from Levi. Away from her safety.

"Stop," she whispered, her throat dry and her grasp on consciousness slipping away. Even her wolf had gone silent, the creature nowhere to be found within her mind. That silence and the unnerving feeling of being alone in her head for the first time in her life sent her into a full panic. Oh God, what had they done? Without her wolf, would she still be mated to Levi? Without that inner spirit, would he feel their connection?

Without her wolf, would she even be herself anymore?

"Can't stop, Armaita. We need to get away while those stupid humans are putting your guard dogs down. That bastard tried to take you, but I tricked him good. You were always supposed to be mine."

Scream!

Amy heard Levi's voice as clear as day in her mind. That one word reminding her how to get his attention. He'd promised he'd come if she screamed for help, but it was too late. She barely had the strength to make a squeak before blackness swirled around her and she lost her tenuous hold on being awake.

Twenty-one

It took about three minutes of being under near-constant fire for Levi to realize the bastards weren't aiming to kill.

"What the fuck is this?" Levi ducked behind a rocking chair as another bullet shattered the handrail near him. The noise made Mammon jerk, but he wasn't conscious enough to hold himself up. He began to slide along the railing as gravity took over. Levi reached out and pulled Mammon back to a sitting position. The guy was practically passed out, something Levi had never seen before.

Phego growled and tucked himself behind the corner of the porch, looking for cover as gunfire sounded every few seconds. "I don't know. They're not coming any closer, but they've got us pinned. You and I could probably make it back inside without being hit, but not Mammon. He's getting worse."

Levi didn't need to agree. They both knew something

was seriously off when a shifter with nothing more than a flesh wound couldn't speak, couldn't move, and couldn't stay conscious. Something was wrong with their friend…with this entire situation.

The men were shooting from behind their car. That was understandable…use a large, bullet-stopping object as cover. It made sense. But they were shooting high and wide, firing every few seconds without rhyme or reason. Either they weren't worried about running out of ammunition, or a direct hit wasn't the overall plan. But then, what would be? A military unit would attack, tighten the net, and eliminate. This was more…attack for attacking's sake.

Phego must have been on the same thought trail.

"Why are they shooting so randomly? It's like these bastards have an endless supply of ammunition or something." Phego jerked as part of the support post exploded. "And whatever they've got on the fucking bullets, it's making Mammon here pretty much useless. Good thing your Amy didn't get hit with one when they shot through the door."

Levi's blood ran cold, and his wolf surged forward. Amy. She'd been bleeding from her arm when he left her inside the house. He didn't know for sure if it was from the glass, the wood of door itself, or the bullets that busted through it all, though. She could be in trouble. She could be half unconscious on the floor, just like Mammon. A thought that made his wolf rage. He reached deep for his mating bond to her, that feeling of *her* in the world around him. Having a mate was still so new, the bond so fragile, but he hunted. He reached.

But he couldn't find it. Couldn't find his sense of her. Anywhere.

"Motherfucker." Levi spun for the door, but the bastards hiding behind their car fired at the wall in front of him, pinning him in place once more. "We need to get to her, to get to the guns. We can take these fuckers out."

Phego growled and tilted his head to look over the handrail. "I know, but the guns are inside, kid."

It was the kid that pushed him right over the edge. Instead of lashing out, though, Levi brought all his anger and frustration inward. A wave of focused attention washed over Levi, slowing down everything around him. He viewed the world as if through a camera lens, marking distance and light, seeking spots of shadow and framing his plan in his head. Opening the aperture, blurring the background until only the most vital pieces of the picture were clear.

"We're going to have to rush them." Every bit of military training Levi had gone through over the centuries fired in his head as the world regained its normal speed. His mate needed him, his brothers needed him, his back was literally to the wall…and he could not fail. If he and Phego were going to get out from under the firepower of these humans, they'd need to remove the threat. That meant taking down the men with the guns.

But Phego didn't jump in with an *affirmative* or *hell yeah* or even a subtle *Ooh Rah*. He just stared as if his pack brother had grown a second head. Something Levi didn't care to think too much about.

"I know it sounds crazy, but we're pinned. Someone is going to have to draw their fire so we can reach our own supplies."

Mammon, seeming at least partially awake all of a sudden, pushed himself off the floor. As the shifter crawled to his knees, wobbly and weak even on all fours, Levi and Phego could only stare. And then the bastard actually spoke.

"Let me."

If there was one thing Levi hadn't expected, it was that.

"You can barely walk."

But Mammon was nothing if not stubborn. "She's your mate, son. You'd die for her, we all know that, but dying's not the best thing to keep her safe right now. They've already shot me once. If this shit clouding my brain is deadly, I'm done for anyway." He leaned closer, his breathing hard as he whispered at Levi. "You take care of that girl. She's way too good for you, kid. You mated up—now earn it."

Mammon offered his arm while looking Levi right in the eye. Understanding and prepared for…whatever was about to happen. Levi accepted the offer, accepted the fact that his brother was prepared to die on behalf of his mate. He didn't balk or beg. He gave the man the respect he deserved for an act so selfless.

Levi gripped Mammon's forearm and nodded once. "I've got your back."

Mammon chuckled. "It's not my back I'm worried about, but I appreciate the effort."

Before he could stand, the roar of a massive piece of machinery blasted through the air. The sound grew louder, more aggressive, as it moved closer. Only one machine made noise like that, and only one Dire Wolf was badass enough to ride the beast.

Levi's relieved sigh was unavoidable. "Here comes the cavalry."

Thaus turned his monster of a Harley onto the gravel drive seemingly without slowing down, one hand holding a handgun nearly the size of his forearm. Holding and aiming.

Levi crept forward to watch the show, waiting for his chance to reach the door. He didn't need much time. Just a brief moment of inattentiveness from the humans. A handful of seconds.

The three humans realized way too late that something

was coming up behind them. Two spun and aimed at the threat, but their shots went wide. Not that a direct hit would have helped. Thaus fired as he drove, leveling his weapon and taking aim with a sniper's focus. He didn't even pause or drop his arm when he slid to a stop and hopped off his bike, firing four times before his feet were on the ground.

The moment the first human spun and fell from the bullet he took, Levi was up and running for the door. He needed to arm his brothers and get to Amy before the other two humans caused any more damage.

His shotgun rested against the wall by the door, exactly where he'd left it. He grabbed the gun on his way past, turning to walk backward into the house while firing. Even through the doorway, his view of the car and the battle outside was perfect—the whole scene almost outlined by the doorframe. He watched as Thaus popped the second human, silently cheering for his brother. But the third—motherfucking Gavin—had moved, had chosen to attack what he probably saw as the easier target. The peeping bastard was running for the porch, aiming straight for Levi's brothers, not noticing the man in the doorway with the shotgun at his shoulder. The one with murder in his eyes. Levi didn't hesitate or second-guess a single damned thing. He sighted down the barrel, took a breath, and popped off a single shot. Gavin jerked and fell backward in a cloud of blood, his gun slipping from his hand and dropping to the ground below him with a satisfying thud.

Done. Almost.

Levi lowered the gun and spun, racing toward the landing where he'd left Amy mere minutes before. Praying to the fates above with every step. He hit the edge of the wall and turned to find… Nothing. The landing was empty, the only remnant of his mate a pool of blood on the hardwood.

Too much blood. The scent crowded out everything else, leaving him unable to track her. And the bond to her, that thread connecting them through their mating bites, was silent and still. Disconnected. Something that threw him into an even deeper wash of panic and rage.

Motherfucking fail.

His heart pounded as he ran through the main floor of the house. Searching every room. Looking inside every closet. When he couldn't find her, he yanked his wolf forward, hoping he at least would be able to track her with more success. He surrendered his human side to the wolf so quickly, he partially shifted instead of going full wolf. His nose lengthening into a half muzzle, his fingers curling into claws. Thick, dark fur sprouted along his arms, shadowing his skin, but he didn't hold it back. Didn't even try to resist. The wolf needed his mate, and he needed his wolf to find her. This would be a shared mission.

Wolf in almost complete control, he snarled and sniffed. Breaking down the mottled odors of the room, seeking to find a way past the smell of gunpowder and blood. He nearly lurched to four feet from two when something sweet registered. There…her scent. Soft and subtle, but present. He tracked it into the kitchen and toward the back door. The *open* back door.

The cold wind blowing inside cleared away the powerful scents that had been covering Amy's. She'd been through here recently, that was for sure. But there was another scent with hers. One of a male shifter. A scent that ignited a memory but didn't allow it to burn long enough to grab hold of. That didn't matter, though. Whoever was with her was a dead man. Levi was getting his mate back. End of discussion.

Phego caught up to Levi just as he stepped out on the back porch. "Mammon's bad, but I think he's actually burning off whatever it is in his blood. He just needs some time to recuperate."

"We don't *have* time."

Phego stepped in front of him, earning a hard glare. "What do you mean? Where's your mate?"

Levi didn't answer right away, didn't even give his brother the respect of looking him in the eye. He couldn't feel his mate through their bond, but he had other ways of finding her. He could smell his mate on the wind, could see the footprints of whoever had her in the snow. One set…in, then out. Someone didn't just take her; they carried her off against her will.

Levi indicated the footprints with his chin. "He's got her."

Thaus rushed out onto the porch, his gun up and ready as he swept the perimeter. "The Omega? Who took her?"

Levi shrugged and set his shotgun against the wall. Casual, probably appearing almost calm even though that was the last thing he felt. Inside, his wolf clawed to be released, ready to rush after the fucker who dared put a hand on his Amy. But Levi took his time, knowing this was it. He was about to go to war with another shifter, one he still couldn't identify, one he knew had tricks up his sleeve… Like being able to get a group of humans to be a living, breathing distraction. Smart, but not smart enough.

"Don't know who. Don't care, either. Someone took my mate." Levi glared at his two Dire brothers, pulling his wolf forward, knowing they'd see the swirling silver in his eyes before his shift came over him. "Whoever he is, whoever dared to touch her? He's about to die."

Levi shifted right there on the porch, his giant wolf form racing for the woods the second his paws touched down. Nothing but instinct and rage left within him. Levi expected support from his brothers, especially from Phego, but it was Thaus who followed him through the snow. The last threads of Levi's human mind were grateful for that fact. Phego could handle helping Mammon heal. Thaus was a beast of a man and a berserker of a wolf, far more aggressive than just about anyone Levi knew.

Whoever had dared to touch one of their own was in for a world of hurt he'd probably never seen coming.

Twenty-two

A sharp jab to her rib cage pulled Amy from the blackness of sleep. She swam for the light, for thought and reason, but her brain remained muddled and groggy. Even through the fog, though, she sensed something wasn't right. The bedroom was too cold, the warmth of her mate wrapped around her missing. And there was a heaviness to her head that was definitely not supposed to be there. Was she… upside down?

Wrong, wrong, definitely something wrong.

But sleep wrapped its icy fingers around her mind again, leading her back into the shadows, and she surrendered to its call.

Seconds later, perhaps hours for all she knew, Amy woke with a start. Still groggy, her thoughts far too slow, still hellishly cold. But this time, she fought the pull of sleep. Fought hard. She took a handful of deeper breaths, the icy air that could only come from being outdoors burning her nose and lungs, in an attempt to try to clear her mind. To stay awake. To figure out what was so wrong about her situation.

And it was definitely very, very wrong.

Upside down, outside, rocking with what felt like the motion of movement from below…all so wrong. The smell of male wolf shifter wafted around her. She inhaled deeper, searching for something to cling to. To recognize. But the scent was not of her mate, a fact that cleared the majority of the fog in her head almost immediately. Pictures, like flashes of memories, filtered through the last of the haze in rapid-fire time. Cabin…breakfast…gunfire…blood…*Zeke*.

Her heart jumped, but she didn't attempt to escape. Didn't even move. The bastard had her tossed over his shoulder like some sort of shifter sack of potatoes, her head dangling halfway down his back as he ran through a patch of woods. He even had his hand on her back as if he was holding her in place. A fact that made her skin crawl.

The instinctive desire to fight until he released her was a big one, but so was the need to know where she was and what was happening first. Plus, it would be nice to have a clear head before she made a mad dash for safety or started swinging. Whatever they'd given her to knock her out had begun to wear off, but it wasn't all gone yet. Her body still felt achy, and her brain wasn't firing as fast as she'd like. But she was alive and awake. True, she was thrown over some man's shoulder as he carted her off to destinations unknown, but she wasn't dead yet. For that, she could be thankful.

As her senses kicked up and her brain cleared even more, she let her thoughts hone in on one thing. Her mate. Her wolf, still near silent in a way that was unnatural, though at least present once more, perked up a bit when she reached for her mating bond. Levi was there, her connection to him still strong and unbroken. Faint, though. Muddied under the drugs or distance. He wasn't close, it seemed, but he also wasn't moving farther away even though Zeke still ran through the woods. That told her he was following them. Probably tracking her, a thought that calmed much of the unease around her. Levi would come for her; he'd help her get away from Zeke.

Amy was pretty sure she could win in a *fair* fight against the shifter, but Zeke had proven he didn't fight fair. The drugs blurring her reality wouldn't help her, either. If she could just figure out a way to stall Zeke, to give Levi a chance to catch up so she had backup, she could take her chance. And she would. No sister of twelve older brothers grew up without knowing how to fight, even if it was just from watching those older boys in their own childish battles.

Amy waited, clinging to that mating thread with all her heart, growing more excited the stronger it became. Levi was closing in. Anytime now, she could begin her escape. As soon as she found a chance.

And then it happened. Fate played into Amy's hand with a steep hill thrown in her way. Or rather, Zeke's way. He stumbled when he hit the incline, his steps slowing and losing their rhythm. Her target was off-balance, headed uphill, and her mate was closing in on them. Time to take what she'd learned by being part of the Bell family and put it to good use.

Amy struck hard and fast from multiple spots. Biting his arm, punching him in the kidneys, and yanking her knees up and into his chest at the same time, not giving Zeke a chance to strike back. The bastard grunted and dropped to his knees, just as she'd expected. She threw her body weight to one side, dropping off his shoulder. A good escape, though not a pretty one. She hit the ground too hard, rolling through the snow in an inelegant sort of flip. May not have gone exactly as planned, but at least Zeke wasn't carrying her anymore. That meant it was time to kick some ass.

But crawling to her knees took longer than it should have, and gaining her feet left her light-headed and woozy. Okay, fine—change of plans. As much as it pissed her off, she turned her back on her captor and stumbled her way down the hill. Levi was definitely closing in and her reaction time wasn't quite back to normal, which meant her smartest move was to avoid engaging Zeke in a fight. She didn't need to escape, really. Okay, fine, she did. But only because of the drugs. Without those, she'd be mopping the forest floor with the bastard. If she could take Abel down—and she had a time or two—she could knock some sense into Zeke. Just… not right then.

Run to Levi, just run to Levi.

"Damn it, Armaita."

Her feet slipped on the hard ground and her head swam with every step, but she continued to put one foot in front of the other. Following the thread she could only sense toward where she knew Levi would be.

She wasn't a fast runner on her best days, and this was not a best day, apparently. She barely made it to the base of the hill before Zeke slammed into her back. She fell forward and slid in the snow, her face on fire from the ice cutting into her cheek. His weight on top of her, his arms encircling her, Zeke had Amy pinned in a matter of seconds. But that didn't stop her from fighting.

Kicking, biting, yelling, punching—having twelve brothers to wrestle with as a child had taught her well. She could break out of a choke hold faster than most shifters, could flip men three times her size if need be, but Zeke was determined to keep her down. Between his sheer will and the hazy mindset that slowed her reflexes, she was losing her fight and fast.

But she wasn't done yet.

Zeke rolled her onto her back, trying to pin her with his weight. Amy kicked harder, bucking her hips to throw him off. Refusing to lie down and take *anything* from him.

"Damn it, Armaita. I'm trying to help you."

She growled and kicked again, hitting him squarely between the legs with her knee. He groaned and curled, giving her the perfect opportunity to toss him off. *Score one for the shewolf.*

"You don't have permission to call me that, and I don't want your kind of help." She struggled to her feet, shaking. It was so cold, and her clothes were wet from rolling around in the snow. She didn't know how long she could make it in her human form, but she wasn't sure she could shift with her mind so fuzzy. Her wolf was still oddly silent—a fact that kept her firmly entrenched in her human side—so she focused on Levi and ran toward where she knew him to be.

She'd taken a mere seven steps when a large wolf she knew had to be Levi raced through the tree line ahead of her. Breathing a sigh of relief, she tried to run faster. Tried to close that distance. Tried to push herself through the snow toward the safety of her mate. Eight steps, nine. Moving faster. Gaining ground.

But it was on her eleventh step that a gun went off.

Twenty-three

Amy.

Levi almost breathed a sigh of relief when he zigged around a copse of trees. She was there—alive and on her own two feet, though she looked a little unstable. She'd somehow gotten away from the skinny shifter who was scrambling on the ice behind her. And then her captor made it to his feet, and Levi's vision went red.

The shifter.

The nomad.

The guy from the bar that night outside of Hope Ridge.

Now, the diner in town? Pure heaven.

The diner's got great food and good company. It can't be beat.

Zeke's words repeated in his head, colored by the knowledge that the shifter had been grooming his mate for some kind of mind-wash-fueled kidnapping. The timing couldn't have been a coincidence, though. Zeke, Gavin, and the two other humans he didn't know had all arrived together. There was reason behind that plan.

Strategy.

Jesus, what had Zeke set up, and how had he gotten *humans* to follow him?

Levi growled deeper and picked up the pace, needing to be by Amy's side. The woman had twelve brothers—there was no way she didn't know how to fight—but that didn't mean he couldn't offer his own brand of help to her. And by help, he meant ripping the threat to pieces and stomping all over the remains. Because that was his plan.

Running hell-for-leather, Thaus raced ahead of him, angling for Zeke as Levi headed straight for Amy. Levi's sole focus was on his mate, though, which was probably why he didn't see the danger coming. Didn't see Zeke rise to his feet and pull something shiny from his waistband. Didn't know there was a gun pointing at his mate until it was too late.

Thaus lunged for Zeke just as the gun went off, but Levi couldn't tear his eyes away from Amy. Her eyes went wide at the sound, and her body jerked then fell forward almost in slow motion. Levi ran the last few steps then shifted without thought, sliding in the snow on his bare knees to catch her before she hit the ground. Her eyes met his for the briefest of moments before she closed them. Pale, skin cold to the touch, she rested in his arms, a fallen angel against a sea of blood-splattered snow.

"Amy." Levi's voice was a prayer to every god ever worshiped, a whispered declaration of need sent out to the universe. The world stood still under the weight of his desperation, and the silence reigned. He curled his naked body around hers and clutched her to him, protecting her, not yet ready to even see if she was still breathing.

But Amy wasn't that patient.

"Levi, let me go." Amy pushed on his shoulders, coughing and kicking to break free. "You'll be okay. It's a weird thing, but it'll wear off. Just calm down."

Levi almost snarled at her for backing away from him, grasping her wrist in a last-ditch effort to keep her close. "What?"

"It'll wear off. There's something with the bullets that makes things fuzzy, but it'll wear off."

Bullets. His mate had been *shot*.

"Okay. Just hold still." Levi jumped and lunged for her, running his hands over her body to find where she'd been hit. Oddly enough, she seemed to be doing the same thing.

"Quit getting in my way," she hissed, pushing his hands away.

"I'm trying to find where you've been shot."

Her eyes went wide, and her hands stilled. "I wasn't hit this time, you were."

The crunch of a footstep on the hard snow had them both spinning. Zeke stood with a handgun pointing their way. But that wasn't the only thing drawing Levi's attention. Thaus lay in the snow a few feet away, silent and still, blood staining the white surface below him red.

Fuck, Zeke must have hit Thaus when the Dire leaped in front of him. But then how—

"She's mine." Zeke stood with one badly damaged arm tucked to his chest, claw marks having sliced all the way to the bone, the gun shaking in his other hand. "I worked for her, set up those human demon hunters to go after her pack so I could get to her, even put up with that lying fucking teacher creeping on her when she was *mine*. You can't have her; I won't let you take Armaita from me."

Levi gently pushed Amy behind him and rose to his feet, keeping his eyes on Zeke. Watching the hand that held the gun without blinking. "Her name's Amy, and she's *my* mate."

Zeke's face turned red, and a low growl rumbled from his chest. "I saw her first."

"Yeah, that's not how this works." Levi kept a hand on Amy's wrist as he edged closer to Zeke. He wanted her to run, to head back to the cabin where Phego could protect her, but he knew she wouldn't. He also knew, if she tried, Zeke would take a shot at her. That wasn't going to happen. He didn't know if the drugs had a cumulative effect or if Zeke was a good enough shot to hit her in the head.

Levi wasn't up to taking chances.

Zeke looked over Levi's shoulder at Amy, a sort of zealous light in his eyes. The look of a man obsessed. "She's mine. I want her."

"Again, that's not how this works. At all." Levi inched closer still, his heart racing, his adrenaline skyrocketing. "She doesn't want you, anyway."

"But she's mine." Zeke dropped his shoulder. Whether the move was in response to sadness or defeat or anger or shock, Levi didn't give a fuck. That drop was his shot. It was just an inch or so, barely enough to notice, but it was the right amount for the barrel of the gun to be aimed more at the ground than him or Amy.

Perfect timing… Levi was sick of the bullshit. "No, Zeke. She's fucking *mine.*"

Levi went full wolf in the middle of his word, kicking off the ground and racing forward before the shift had actually completed. It was a brazen move, he knew, but the only chance he'd get. He needed to disarm Zeke, and he needed to get it done immediately.

Luckily, speed and surprise were on his side. Zeke barely had time to growl before Levi hit him. The force of Levi's head connecting squarely with the smaller man's chest knocked Zeke right off his feet. Levi didn't let up, though. He clamped down on the shifter's wrist, tearing through flesh and breaking bones, making sure the gun fell before he continued his attack. Zeke's pained screams broke the silence of the winter forest, but Levi didn't care. He snarled louder, bit harder, and slashed at his enemy with a single-minded purpose.

Protect Amy.

This ended—Zeke's life ended—right there in the woods. Levi would make sure of it.

Twenty-four

Amy knelt in the snow, her head hanging and her tears freezing to her cheeks. The sounds of the fight between Levi and Zeke were something out of her nightmares, but she didn't run. She couldn't. The wolf who'd raced with Levi to help her was in trouble. It had to be one of Levi's pack, maybe even one of the ones she'd met. The ones she'd fed.

One of his brothers.

If it were one of *her* brothers bleeding out on the snow, she'd want someone to help him. She'd beg for it. So instead of running away to safety, she scooted closer to the fallen wolf. Closer to the fight.

Blood stained the ground in a macabre sort of polka-dot pattern. The white snow had turned a nauseating shade of pink from the scuffle of paws, though there were still large spots of red all around. Those spots grew in size and number as Levi treated his prey like a chew toy. Zeke's dark wolf was bleeding horribly, which was a good sign for her mate.

And Levi…

He was huge in his wolf form. Huge and spotted in a way she'd never seen. As was his fallen brother. Both heavily muscled, built for fighting and obviously skilled at battle with a rough air about them that spoke of violence. Levi and this man were protectors, for sure. Soldiers, even. But the one had fallen.

Amy crawled right up to the wolf's side, pushing past the fear he instilled. He'd been shot in the shoulder; a wound she knew would be hard to reset simply because of all the moving pieces that controlled motion. Shifters healed well and quickly, but that didn't mean they'd always heal exactly as they should. She could still hear the screaming from her brother Caleb when he had to have his leg broken a third time because of a knee injury. That night had ended with all thirteen men in her family growing damp in the eye, though they'd never admit it. Still, if Caleb could handle that level of pain and come back from it—he barely even limped anymore—this hulking beast could deal. She just needed to help him.

The wolf on the ground growled as she inched closer. The sound was muffled and weak, not at all what she expected from an animal his size. A sure sign that he was dazed and in pain. Still, the rumble built on an instinctual fear that was hard to fight back.

"I won't hurt you." She crept closer, keeping an eye on his front legs. The weapons at the ends were a ridiculous bastardization of wolf claws—long and thick, obviously sharp, and ready to slice someone open with a single swipe. He looked too weak to attack—or so she hoped—but he continued to growl louder and harsher as she approached. The noise went from slightly scary to downright annoying, though, as it piled on top of the sounds of her mate fighting behind her. Plus, it wasn't helping him in any way. Why was he growling at her when he should have been resting so he could heal faster? Stubborn fool of a man, this one. Amy had dealt with a few of those in her lifetime. Like twelve or so.

Which meant she knew exactly how to treat him, larger size and scariness be damned.

"You can either keep growling and lose the energy you need to heal, or you can be smart and stop. Doesn't matter to me. I'm taking care of you either way."

The wolf went quiet, but his eyes—those unusual, molten-silver eyes—stayed wary and watchful. She had a feeling this wasn't Phego or Mammon, though she couldn't put her finger on how she knew that. Perhaps it was in the way the beast refused to trust her. Or maybe it was the blank stare. Levi's brothers had been lively and personable, scary in a way but kind to her. This one…he was none of those things. He was pure aggression, and even fallen as he was, that will to fight was something she sensed on the air. Like a warning or a threat. He'd given her an inch, but that was it. She wasn't going to be allowed a sliver more.

And yet, she had to *take* more from him if she was going to help him survive.

Without hesitation, she yanked off her wet T-shirt and rolled it into a ball. The garment wasn't the best option, but it was the only thing she had. She placed the sodden fabric against where the wolf was bleeding the most. And then she pushed hard to slow the deluge.

His whimper of pain rolled straight into a snarl that made the hair on the back of her neck stand on end.

"Sorry, but I have to stop the bleeding." She shrugged, trying not to think of how cold the wind was as it blew across her damp skin, thankful his eyes hadn't left her face. At least he wasn't staring at her bra-clad chest. That would be awkward, which wasn't really what she needed to be worried about when a wolf who could probably slice her in half with one kick was right in front of her. "The shirt's probably cold, but it's the only thing I have right now. As soon as Levi's finished with Zeke, we'll get you back to the cabin and find real supplies."

As soon as Levi was finished. Meaning, as soon as Levi killed the other shifter. Amy swallowed back the sick feeling in her stomach. She'd never thought of herself as violent, never imagined a time when she would treat the death of another shifter so casually. But Zeke had crossed too many lines. He'd lied, schemed, stalked, and attacked her.

Amy's family, her entire pack, really, were blunt and direct. You knew from the get-go what you were going to get with them. Zeke wasn't like that. He'd tricked her, and that trickery could have cost her the mate she'd only just found. It also could have put her entire pack in danger, what with him working with humans. The shifter deserved whatever justice Levi dished out.

A sharp whimper pulled her from her thoughts. She flinched and jerked away from her patient, whispering a soft, "Sorry."

But the wolf below her didn't move, didn't even bother to look at her. He stared past her hip, watching something behind her.

Levi.

The forest had gone almost silent, the sounds of fighting over, not even the impression of a death knell whispering through the trees. Something she hadn't noticed until that moment.

Amy closed her eyes and took a deep breath, digging for her connection to her mate. He was there, his essence deep inside of her. His aggression strong in the vibrations. He was

there, and he was pissed. But he was also feeling a little…
triumphant.

She spun with her heart in her throat, verifying what she already knew from her bond, and then she sighed.

The whimper hadn't come from Levi but from Zeke. The smaller shifter was completely overpowered, his body fallen and pinned under that of her mate. Levi had his teeth in Zeke's throat, his fur bristling along his spine, his claws embedded in the other wolf's ribs. Zeke would be done soon. The long, gaping wounds along his torso and the pool of red underneath his head and shoulders proved that. A shifter couldn't survive that amount of blood loss.

Levi, in all his muscled, mottled glory, wasn't even fighting anymore. He waited instead, patiently listening for the last beat of a heart. A soldier intent on finishing his mission.

The wolf under her hands tried to move, so she spun back around and pressed harder against the shirt. Too relieved to keep the smile out of her voice. "Hold still. The bullets had something on them that slowed your healing. You'll bleed more if you move around."

His eyes met hers—bright like liquefied metal. Silver eyes, dark spots on their flanks, large and muscled and scary even to their own kin. These men weren't normal pack wolves. There was something special about them, something different.

"What are you?"

The creak of footfalls on snow pulled her attention back to the fight. Or what was the fight. Zeke lay still in the snow, not moving, a circle of blood beneath him that told Amy all she needed to know. Levi had succeeded. Her mate in his wolf form stood to the side of the fallen man, sniffing, looking him over as if to verify the threat was eliminated. To make sure she was again safe.

Amy turned back to his fallen brother, knowing her mate wouldn't stop until he was positive the danger had passed. She sat with the wolf instead, pressing on his wounds and watching his chest rise and fall with every breath.

Eventually, Levi's warm arms wrapped around her, acting as a balm to her anxious soul. She leaned into his embrace, wanting to feel more of him against her. Relaxing even as the wolf below watched her with those dangerous eyes.

"Is he okay?"

Amy smiled down at the wolf. "He'll be fine once the drugs wear off. The shoulder wound is messy but not life-threatening. A few more minutes of rest, and then we can see about getting him up, I think."

"Okay. A few minutes is good, because while we need to get back and check on the others, you wanted to know what he is. What…we both are." Levi kissed her neck and pulled her tight. "Dire Wolves. The biggest, the wildest, and the oldest of the wolf shifters. A slightly different breed long thought extinct by your kind." He took what felt like a deep breath, a slight growl rumbling through him, vibrating against her back. "My brothers and I, we're the last of them. Seven men of the Dire line left in the world, though we can't tell anyone that fact. Our safety relies on keeping our secret."

The wolf stared up at her, as if weighing her response. Amy kept her hands pressing her shirt against his wound, kept her eyes on his.

"I've never heard of a Dire Wolf before."

"We try not to be overtly…visible."

Amy looked over her shoulder at her handsome mate, intrigued by his story but still just so damn grateful he was alive. "How have you stayed hidden for so long?"

"We don't really hide. Most packs have forgotten the

legends, or they assume the extinction tales are correct so they never expect to see a Dire Wolf. They don't think anything about our appearance when we shift in front of them. We also have platoons of men under us—regular shifters—who can step into a mission should our true identities need to stay under wraps."

"Huh." Dire Wolves. She was mated to one. She had the blood of another all over her. How strange her world had become. And yet, there were things to do. Realities to deal with. The first being the wolf before her and his injuries. Amy pulled the shirt away from his shoulder wound to check it, satisfied when the blood no longer flowed freely. "We can try to get him up now, I think.

Levi must have expected a more dramatic reaction from her. "Hang on a second… Just 'huh'?"

The wolf cocked an eyebrow, almost challenging her in some way. Waiting for an answer. Amy bit her lip, accepting her feelings for what they were. No, not just "huh," but she was cold, she was wet, and she had the blood of someone important to her mate all over her. Out of all the things she could have freaked out about, the fact her mate was some sort of almost mystical subset of shifter wasn't anywhere close to the top of the list.

Giving the wolf an eyebrow raise worthy of one of her brothers' dumb moves, Amy replied, "I would have liked for you to tell me this sooner, but it's not like your being a Dire Wolf is going to change fate."

Her words sounded even more true spoken out loud than they had in her head. They sounded right. She leaned into Levi's shoulder and tilted her head for a kiss. "You're still my mate; you're just way cooler is all."

Levi chuckled but granted her request, kissing her softly before pulling back with a sigh. "Our belief is that Omegas are the last females of the Dire line as well. We get size and strength—you Omegas get the power to hold a pack together."

"Lucky me."

"The luck's all mine with this one." He kissed her again, longer this time, making her almost forget how cold she was. Almost. Eventually, though, he pulled away, squeezing her tighter in his arms. "How's my brother here?"

"I'm not entirely sure…he's awfully quiet." Amy shivered, clenching her jaw to keep her teeth from rattling. "He's going to have a rough go until that shoulder heals, though. We may need to build some sort of sled to get him back."

"Doubtful." Levi inched forward, practically leaning around her. "Thaus, this is my mate, Armaita, though she prefers Amy. Amy, meet Thaus. He's one of my Dire brothers, and the second-baddest motherfucker I've ever met. Give him a minute, and he'll probably be able to pull *us* back to the cabin."

"Second-baddest? That sounds ominous." Amy shivered, the cold truly seeping into her bones. "And a minute's about all I've got left out here."

Levi ran his hands over her arms. "Jesus, you're so cold. Why don't you shift, doll?"

"But, your brother—"

"Don't worry about anything with Thaus. Just go wolf and be warm."

The thought of her wolf form, of the heavy fur that would cover her weaker human self, tempted her. But still… "Are you sure?"

"Absolutely." He leaned closer to whisper in her ear. "I want to see your wolf form. I bet you have a great tail."

Amy couldn't help but laugh. "You're such a perv."

"Just for you." He bit her shoulder, inciting a growl that surprised even her. The wolf on the ground huffed what sounded like a snort, snagging Amy's attention once more.

Levi sighed. "You hush, old man."

"All right, you two. I'm shifting before I start losing body parts to this cold."

Levi leaned back on his palms to watch her, completely naked. Comfortable in his skin. He was so damned handsome, so stunning in his masculinity. Amy wanted to straddle him and give him one more deep kiss, to rub her body against his and check every single inch of him to be sure he was okay after the fight. But the wind whipped across the clearing, stinging her eyes and making her skin burn. There would be time alone with her naked mate later. For now, she needed not to die of hypothermia.

Amy stepped away and shifted, letting her wet clothes fall to the ground. With her four paws on the snow, she shook from the tip of her nose to the end of her tail. It felt good to be in her wolf form; it felt right. And it was so much warmer.

"I was right." Levi grinned, giving her a wink. "You've got a great tail."

Amy snorted a laugh and pranced across the snow. Might as well give the man a bit of a show, after all. She rubbed against Levi's back as he laughed at her antics, nuzzling into his neck, hoping to share some warmth.

Thaus huffed again before pushing up to a sitting position. He wasn't exactly what she'd call stable, but he was able to stay upright. A definite improvement. Levi had his arm extended, ready to catch his friend if need be. Amy rushed to Thaus' other side, using her body to hold his up. Pressing herself against him without thought to his innate stay-the-fuck-away-ness.

Thaus didn't pull away from her, but he certainly didn't seem to want her touching him. He made a sound close to a whine before growling. Loudly.

"Give in to it, man," Levi said as he got to his feet. "She's sort of amazing. She'll win even you over. Hell, she had Mammon saying *thanks* and *ma'am* this morning."

Thaus turned his head to eye her. He was so much bigger than she was, so much taller. There was no way she could ever compete with him and win, so she let her tongue loll out of her mouth and gave him what could only be called a doggy grin. He could be scary and she could be silly. Let him try to be grumpy; she'd find his good mood. If he even had one.

Which she doubted.

With a huff, Thaus rose to all four feet. He wobbled on the first step, nearly fell on the second, but the rest seemed to come easy. Still, Amy stayed by his side. Levi shifted and walked slightly behind them, keeping a watchful eye on the woods. Guarding the weaker wolves. The act was something she appreciated and respected him for. Amy didn't think she or Thaus could handle another attack.

Close to an hour later when the three finally made it back to the cabin, they found Mammon awake in the living room. He was still pale, but he wasn't dead. Which was good news considering Amy and Thaus had been hit with the same drugged bullets.

Phego was nowhere to be found, but Amy had bigger things to worry about. Bigger as in Thaus. He'd shifted from wolf to man in the hallway and stumbled to the couch. He fell in an arc, flipping in midair to land on his back. An impressive feat, but not as impressive as his physicality. He was completely naked, as she expected him to be. That was normal. The layers of muscle covering his body weren't, nor was the size of his…him.

"Cover yourself, for fuck's sake." Levi tossed a blanket over Thaus' lap, glaring, his shoulders stiff. Amy, still in her wolf form, ducked behind him and pressed against his calves. She needed to feel him close to her. Was desperate for some time alone with him to decompress after everything. Even on four feet, she felt more wobbly than normal. Her adrenaline crash was going to be epic.

Thaus, in all his naked glory, simply raised an arm and extended a finger. A middle one.

"Another fucking mated Dire," Thaus said with a growl. Amy glanced up at Levi, who winked at her. Yep. Mated. Which meant he probably felt how on edge she was. He knew. And she had no doubt he'd help her through it.

With a chuff to her mate, she trotted into the bedroom to shift and find some clothes. She had a feeling Levi wouldn't like her walking around naked in front of the other men, even if that was the shifter way.

Her naked mate followed her a few minutes later, pressing himself against her back the second he walked into the room. Covering her with his body and holding her up with his strong arms.

"I'm so sorry Zeke touched you." Levi's voice was dark and gritty, wrought with emotions she could only guess at. Even with their connection, she knew he was only allowing her access to the shallowest of his sensations. The man was shaking against her, growling softly as his hands explored. As he checked to be sure she was okay.

He was a man coming undone, and she *knew*… She sensed it. He needed her to help hold him together.

"I'm okay." She turned, fisting her hands in his hair and pulling him down to her. "We're all going to be okay."

Levi shook his head, pinching his eyes closed. "I should

have—"

"Stop it." She forced herself to glare when his eyes popped open to meet hers. "No could haves, should haves, or would haves. You did what you thought was right in the moment."

He sighed and pulled her closer, squeezing her almost to the point of pain. "I could have lost you."

The agony and fear in his voice nearly broke her heart. "But you didn't. I'm right here. And this whole thing…it's over. The bad guys are all gone."

Levi's shoulders stiffened. "Well, not *all* of them."

Amy leaned back and raised her eyebrows, waiting.

Levi shrugged. "Phego's questioning one of the humans now. We need to know what Zeke had going on and who knew about it. We have to make sure there's no one else looking for you."

Phego…busy. Thaus…healing on the couch. "What about Mammon?"

Levi cocked his head, looking down at her in question. "He's passed out upstairs."

Amy hummed and slid her hands down along his neck and over his shoulders. "So, we have some time?"

His growl deepened, his body responding to her touch. "We do. A few hours, probably. Phego likes his job." He leaned in and nibbled up the length of her neck, his hands gripping her hips and pulling her against where he was already hard for her. "We should probably talk. Maybe make some plans for our future."

But his hands were gripping her hips and his hard dick was nestled against her stomach. "I'd rather do something other than talk."

Levi growled all low and sexy. Needful. "Did you have anything specific in mind?"

Amy shrugged. "Well, I am naked…"

Levi grinned, a smirky, arrogant sort of smile. And then Amy was airborne. She landed on the mattress with a jolt, laughing as her mate crawled on top of her.

"What are we doing?" She reached for him, pulling him up to her, wanting to feel his weight. He nuzzled into her neck, biting down hard on the muscles there before licking his way to her ear.

"Fucking."

Amy shivered and moaned, spreading her legs around his hips. Ready to reconnect with her mate in the best way she could. "Sounds like a plan to me."

Epilogue

Levi followed Amy up the steps, staying close but not too close. He loved watching that ass sway even if he could only see it because of his wolf vision. Nighttime in the mountains was no joke.

"Are you sure about this?" She looked so nervous, it was almost comical.

"I'm sure." Levi nudged her toward the door. It'd been almost a full day since he'd had her in his arms. The drive back to Hope Ridge ended up taking longer than expected because of a snowstorm, and her constant sexiness had been ramping him up the entire way. He needed her alone, bare, and underneath him in about three-point-five seconds or he was going to explode.

And yet she still stalled. "But you're used to being more solitary. You don't know what life here is like. We're talking a lot of—"

"I know. You've told me. I'm still in." Another nudge

and a growl to make his point. As much as he loved her voice, she needed to stop talking and move. He really didn't want to strip her naked right there on the porch in the dark, in the middle of what was shaping up to be a goddamned blizzard.

The wind kicked up, sending snow spiraling around them, proving his silent point. Levi kept his focus on Amy's hand, or rather, the keys she held. If she'd just grab the right one and stick it in the lock, things could get started. That's all he needed—an unlocked door. Otherwise, he would bust the fucker down. Just like the back door he'd busted through the night he first met her. The night his life had changed for the better.

"I don't want our relationship to be all about me." She sighed, oblivious to how close he was to the edge.

"I do."

That little glare was adorable. And sexy. Seriously, the girl needed to stop stalling and get them in her house. He was going to fuck her six ways from Sunday as soon as they got inside, hopefully for a couple of days. He knew she needed to get back to the diner and work, but he wanted to be selfish with her time. Of course, when she went back to work, he'd be going with her until the next mission came up. There had to be something he could do to help her in that diner. Plus, the hardware store sat right across the street. The hardware store that could duplicate the key that would get them into the house. If he'd had a key, they'd already be inside. Unclothed. He'd have her on her stomach, pinned down and writhing underneath him as he—

Amy shook her head, her scent rising above the cold smell of snow on the air. "You have no idea—"

And he was done.

"Armaita." Levi pressed her to the door, making sure to

rub his hard cock against her hip to let her know just what was waiting for her.

"Yeah." Her eyes were wide, he voice soft. Breathy. He had her attention for sure.

The howl of a wolf in the mountains above them broke the steady buzz of the wind whipping around them. More joined the first, creating a wall of sound rarely heard outside of the wildest parts of the world. Amy pulled away, her head turning to look toward the mountains. A smile on her pretty face.

"They're welcoming us home."

"Good." Levi licked up her neck, letting the song of his wolfy brethren soothe his anxious soul. "So long as they don't come down here for a few hours."

Amy sighed, trying so hard to sound annoyed but belying her exaggerated breathing with the way her hips rocked into his every few seconds. "They'll interrupt us at some point."

"Not yet."

"Soon."

"Amy, stop." Levi leaned in and kissed her nose, staring into her beautiful eyes as he let his truth come out.

"I know you have twelve brothers, a pack, and a business here. I know this is your home and not something I helped you pick out, and that it implies a permanency I've avoided until this point in my life. I know that choosing to move here, to this little town in the mountains of North Carolina, means bringing all the drama of a big family and an existence intermingled with humans to my doorstep. Trust me, *I know*." Levi growled and grabbed her hand. The one with the keys. The one that had an important job to do if they were going to move things along. "What I don't know is why we're still talking about it when we could be inside that door and naked already."

He shook her hand, making the keys rattle. She blinked then pulled her wrist from his grasp and dropped her arm. She must have managed to get the key into the lock without looking because, with a twist of her arm, the door opened. They stumbled inside, him still trying to stay attached to her. She backed away with a look in her eyes that spoke of all sorts of delicious things to come. That was definitely a look he liked.

"Where are you going?" Levi asked, making sure his voice was deep and growly. Stalking toward her.

"Kitchen. I thought you might be hungry." That teasing grin she wore was something he hadn't seen before. And he liked it. So did his aching cock.

Levi unfastened his jeans and pulled himself out, stroking from base to tip as he kept his eyes on hers. "Oh, I'm hungry, all right."

Amy's eyes flicked down, and her tongue peeked out to wet her full bottom lip. "Do you want me…to cook?" She cocked her head, her lips turning up. She knew what she was doing to him with that pause. Knew exactly how her teasing was affecting him.

"I definitely want you," he said, growling louder as he flicked the ridge of his cock with his thumb. "But not to cook."

Levi lunged with a snarl and grabbed her, pulling her closer by the arm as he stroked himself. Loving the way she couldn't stop staring at his hand. "I want to get you out of those clothes. Then I want to throw you on the bed. Then I want to have my tongue inside you for at least a week."

"A week, huh? Without a good meal to give you sustenance that might be a problem."

"Oh, I'll eat." Levi licked the length of her neck and flicked her earlobe. "I'll eat until you can't stop screaming."

She giggled and gripped his shoulders, pulling him with her as she walked backward toward the bedroom. "You're so dirty."

"You like it."

"Hell yeah, I do."

Hours later, Levi stumbled from the bed to find her. It definitely wouldn't be hard to do—the smell of bacon coming from the kitchen was a dead giveaway.

"I'd say I need to work harder at wearing you out, but I'm starving and that smells amazing."

Amy turned and smiled, almost knocking him on his ass. She was so fucking beautiful standing at the stove and wearing one of his T-shirts—the cotton hugging her curves and barely covering her ass. She had a towel over one shoulder and a set of tongs in her hand. Sexy fucking chef surrounded by the smell of bacon. She looked like some sort of domestic wet dream. *His* domestic wet dream.

"I figured breakfast was in order after that performance."

Levi couldn't resist a second more. He crept up behind her, nuzzling into her neck and running his hand under the shirt to cup her ass as he pulled her against him. "So I get rewarded for good sex with bacon? I can live with that."

She smacked his chest and shooed him to the table, where he spent the next ten minutes watching her in her element. A beautiful and intriguing sight, one he hoped to see on a daily basis from then on.

"Will Thaus be okay?" Amy asked as she brought the food to the table.

Levi kissed her hand in thanks before grabbing a piece of bacon. "Phego said his shoulder's pretty messed up, but they've got a shifter doc making sure it heals as well as it can. I'm not overly worried—he's tough. They'll get him straightened out."

Amy took a bite of her pancakes, chewing silently as she stared blankly at the table. Her mind was somewhere else, that much was obvious. That much Levi could tell. So he waited her out, giving her a chance to collect her thoughts while he devoured his bacon and pancakes.

He didn't have to wait too long.

"I can't believe Zeke convinced humans of our existence. Why would he do that?"

Levi set his fork down as his stomach knotted. Zeke didn't just tell humans of shifter existence. He convinced them shifters were all demons from hell and needed to be destroyed. All to get his hands on Amy. Zeke had planned to let the humans kill off her entire pack, leaving her alone and helpless so he could swoop in and rescue her. But Abel finding that scent trail and figuring out people were in the woods had thrown a wrench in his plans. When Levi thought about all that could have gone wrong if Abel had never noticed the trail, if the pack had never called for help, if he hadn't chosen the assignment and come north—

"What's wrong?"

Levi glanced up, meeting Amy's concerned eyes. He didn't want her worrying, especially not right then. They had good food in front of them, good sex behind them, and more good sex on the horizon. It was not the time to worry but to celebrate.

He shook his head, letting go of the could have beens and focusing on the now. Because he *had* gotten the call for help, *had* come north for the mission, *had* followed that trail, and *had* found his mate. He'd killed the threat to her, and Phego had taken care of the last human who knew the secret of her pack.

"Nothing's wrong."

Amy gave him a look that said she didn't believe him.

He shrugged again and smiled. "Nothing's wrong at all, doll."

And it wasn't. Not really. But he wouldn't be leaving Amy's side until he made sure she was safe. Already, his tech expert Dire brother Deus was on his way to wire her little house and business for a full security system. Levi would have to explain everything about that to her later, as well as the fact that she'd be getting a different cell phone. One with a tracker ID in it and above-standard encryption. She was an Omega and mated to a Dire Wolf, which made her part of their pack. Dire Wolves protected their own above all else.

Nope, nothing was wrong…and it would stay that way once her home and business were wired, the town was monitored, and Levi joined his little life with her big one. Because that was his plan—move to her tiny town in the mountains, set up a safe house for the Dires, and live happily ever after with his mate. Or, at least, sexily ever after. Speaking of which…

"You've got three minutes to finish your breakfast."

Amy looked up, her fork hovering in midair, her brow furrowed. "What's happening in three minutes?"

Levi grinned and said nothing, watching the clock. Amy, obviously a little peeved at his refusal to answer, went back to her breakfast with a huff. She wouldn't be mad for long, though. At the three-minute mark, Levi set his napkin on his plate and slid beneath the table. He heard her breath catch as he spread her knees with his shoulders. Felt her pulse pick up as he yanked her ass to the edge of her seat and pushed her chair back so he could work.

"Levi." She gasped and bucked when he slid two fingers

inside of her.

But he didn't respond. He was too busy staring, devouring her with his eyes. He craved her, needed to taste her. So he did. Diving in without preamble or preparation. Growling at the way she moaned and grabbed his hair as he sucked on her flesh.

"I said I wanted a week with my tongue inside you." Tongue…fingers…cock. All of him. He wanted to get lost in her for days, wanted to leave her a sweaty, sated mess. He wanted a life with his mate, wherever she chose to be, so long as she dragged him along with her. He wanted that happily ever after he'd never known could really exist, and he was going to take it.

So he went to work on his first promise…and his third… and his fourth.

A Dire Wolves MISSION

Also *Available*

FERAL BREED MOTORCYCLE CLUB
Claiming His Fate
Claiming His Need
Claiming His Witch
Claiming His Beauty
Claiming His Fire
Claiming His Desire

FERAL BREED FOLLOWINGS
Claiming His Chance
Claiming His Prize
Claiming His Grace

THE GATHERING
Killian & Lyra
Gideon & Kalie
Blasius, Dante, & Moira
Blasius, Dante, & Moira: Homecoming

About the Author

A storyteller from the time she could talk, Ellis grew up among family legends of hauntings, psychics, and love spanning decades. Those stories didn't always have the happiest of endings, so they inspired her to write about real life, real love, and the difficulties therein. From farmers to werewolves, store clerks to witches—if there's love to be found, she'll write about it. Ellis lives in the Chicago area with her husband, daughters, and to tiny fish that take up way too much of her time.

www.ellisleigh.com